PIRATES, BATS, AND DRAGONS

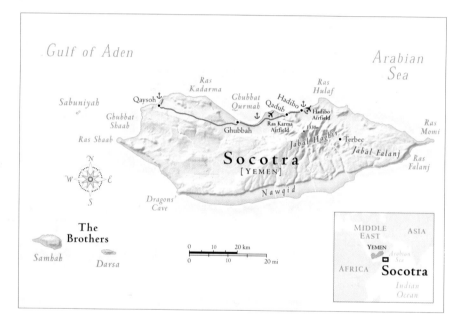

c o d a

Between Suqutra and Hafun's head,
Pray your course be never set . . .
ANCIENT SEA VERSE[1]

I know not a more singular spot on the whole
surface of the globe than the island of Socotra.
LT. J. R. WELLSTED (1840)[2]

Suqutra had always been unattainable.
TIM MACKINTOSH-SMITH (2001)[3]

⌘⌘⌘

PIRATES, BATS, AND DRAGONS

⋟ A SCIENCE ADVENTURE ⋞

MIKE DAVIS

ILLUSTRATIONS BY
WILLIAM SIMPSON

ℙ ERCEVAL PRESS

ISLANDS MYSTERIOUS
Where Science Rediscovers Wonder

PART I
LAND OF THE LOST MAMMOTHS

PART II
PIRATES, BATS, AND DRAGONS

PART III
forthcoming October 2005

XOXOX

PIRATES, BATS, AND DRAGONS

ISBN 0-9747078-2-1
© 2004 Perceval Press
© 2004 Text Mike Davis
© 2004 Illustrations William Simpson

First Edition

Published by Perceval Press
1223 Wilshire Blvd., Suite F
Santa Monica, CA 90403
www.percevalpress.com

Editors: Pilar Perez and Viggo Mortensen
Design: Michele Perez
Copy Editor: Sherri Schottlaender
Cartography by David Deis

Printed in Spain at Jomagar, S/A

Distributed to the book trade
by Publishers Group West

CONTENTS

CHAPTER ONE: *Collision Course*

I should see Soqotra, the ominous island which everyone is afraid of,
in about four days. Apparently they shoot at passing boats and there
was an incident of piracy reported here just a few weeks ago.
I hope to sneak by unseen in the darkness of the night.

LOG OF THE YACHT *NANOU*[4]

Another miniature flying vehicle, an ornithopter dubbed Microbat,
is in development. In its final form, Microbat is expected to weigh
less than fifteen grams, including controls and a miniature
camera with downlink capability.

AEROVIRONMENT PRESS RELEASE (2003)

1. OFF SOCOTRA

2100 hours. Lat. 12° 52' N. Long. 54° 2' E. Northeast of Socotra Island; Gulf of Aden. 17.2 knots. Seas moderate. Lightning squalls on the western horizon. Ship on full alert. Accommodation block locked down and deck patrol posted.

The captain of the *Ryukyu Rainbow* relished the old-fashioned ritual of penning entries into his logbook. Although the position of his 34,000-ton product tanker was hourly uplinked to a satellite and broadcast to the home office in Yokohama, the captain's log was a reassuring holdover of maritime tradition. It evoked an age before automated engine rooms, computerized navigation, shipboard fax machines, and, for that matter, pirates rocketing across the sea in 900-horsepower speedboats.

The *Ryukyu Rainbow* had entered the most dangerous waters in the world: the eastern approaches to the Red Sea around the legendary island of Socotra. During the southwest monsoon season, Suez-bound shipping was menaced by typhoons and monster seas. During the other half of the year, ships were prey for local pirates, criminal syndicates, and international terrorists. In recent years dozens of ships had been boarded and robbed, or hijacked, with their crews held for ransom. (Worldwide, modern piracy is an estimated $16 billion-per-year business.) More ominously, some had simply disappeared without a trace.

With a load of aviation fuel aboard equivalent to a small atomic bomb, the captain was taking no chances. His crew had been practicing the antipiracy drill all week. The ship's superstructure was floodlit, fire hoses were rigged on the aft deck to repel boarders, and the engine room was locked down. Radar ceaselessly swept the flanks of the vessel, but there was a blind spot—actually the shadow of the ship's stack—at the stern. The captain remembered a warning from a previous victim: "They always attack from the stern."

At 2200 the watch changed. The captain—a seafarer with a prophetic ulcer—returned to his cabin to retrieve some pills. The intercom stopped him in the gangway. "Captain, something astern is weaving in and out of our radar."

He rushed to the poop deck, but it was too late—there were grappling hooks over railings. A tall Somali pirate wearing a tattered Oakland Raiders T-shirt was pointing a Kalashnikov at a tiny Filipino crew member. Several more pirates were climbing up the transom. One had an RPG7 rocket launcher swinging from his back, while another, incongruously, was wearing a yellow raincoat.

The pirates were cool and professional, almost polite. The crew surrendered without resistance: a single stray bullet might ignite 19,000 tons of A1 jet fuel. The resulting explosion probably would be visible from space. A crewman struggled to explain the danger to the pirates, but they ignored him.

The interlopers forced the captain to unlock the crew cabins, which they then efficiently stripped of cash, watches, rings, passports, CD players, and even athletic shoes. The loot was stowed in duffel bags and lowered to the waiting speedboat.

The pirates padlocked everyone in the officers' mess. The captain reassured the crew that the automatic navigation system would keep them safely on course until the engineers—five levels below and totally oblivious of the piracy—managed to figure out that something was wrong.

The pirates were disembarking when their leader, in sheer afterthought, decided he should knock out the radios on the bridge. Bounding up the metal stairs three steps at a time, he forced his way into the wheelroom and opened up wildly for ten or fifteen seconds with his AK-47. Satisfied that he had wiped out the ship's communications system, he leisurely made his way back to the poop deck. Taking a final souvenir, he stole the large Japanese merchant flag from the stern.

The pirates sped away at fifty knots toward the lightning on the horizon. Their intent had been simple robbery, but in blasting the ship's radios the pirate leader had also inadvertently destroyed the GPS-based automatic navigation system. The *Ryukyu Rainbow* was effectively pilotless and rudderless.

Somewhere ahead, at the convergence of two powerful currents, were the deadly rocks of Ras Momi on the east coast of Socotra.

2. THE SWARM

Ten thousand miles away, the campus of the California Institute of Technology was basking in gorgeous January sunshine. Jack Davis was on the roof of the Guggenheim Aeronautical Laboratory adjusting the fine focus on a small but powerful cassegrainian telescope. It was aimed at the snowy peak of Mt. Wilson, twelve miles distant. Dr. Lagarde, his aeronautics advisor, and Dr. Graham, from planetary sciences, were standing next to him.

The scrutiny of the two eminent professors made Jack nervous, so he tried to distract himself with a pleasant thought. He conjured an image of his younger brother back home in Ireland, dissecting some frozen mammoth specimen in an unheated basement lab at University College Dublin. "Brrrr . . . poor Conor," he chuckled to himself.

"Much longer, Jack?" Dr. Lagarde jolted him back to Pasadena.

Just then Jack's cell phone rang. It was his lab mate and partner in crime, Sebastian Chen.

"Jack, we're armed and dangerous at this end. How about you?"

"Gimme a few seconds, Sebastian."

Jack peered through his eyepiece. Mt. Wilson jumped at him. On its summit was the famous Carnegie Observatory, and at the foot of the 100-inch reflector was a small orange speck: It was Sebastian in his ski parka.

"OK, Sebastian, activate the guidance laser."

A tiny brilliant red thread was silhouetted against the dome of the observatory.

"Jack, we're locked to trajectory."

He bit his lip and crossed his fingers. The moment of truth had arrived. "Do or die, Sebastian. Unleash the swarm."

"Ten seconds to launch," was the reply from Mt. Wilson. "Nine, eight . . ."

Jack's stomach churned uneasily. Dr. Lagarde cast a doubtful glance at Dr. Graham, who shook his head. Their lack of confidence didn't bode well.

At stake were eighteen months of black coffee at 3 A.M.; hundreds of hours toiling in the microaerodynamics lab with Sebastian; dozens of student parties, films, and hiking trips declined—all for the sake of a tiny obsession.

If the experiment succeeded, Jack was free to spend a semester on another overseas adventure with his brother and their friend Julia. But if it failed—as his advisors seemed to expect—then he and Sebastian were dog meat: demoted from the honors program, back to the dreary undergraduate grind of differential equations and three-hour exams.

"Launch!"

Jack's computer screen was suddenly filled with flashing colored arrows. He pushed a function key, and a huge flat monitor screen in front of Dr. Graham illuminated. It was divided into a dozen empty squares.

Jack gulped. "Sebastian, there's no downlink."

"Oops, sorry." Nine of the monitor cells instantly filled with moving images of the chaparral-covered slopes of Mt. Wilson.

"Three of the bats are black."

"One's dead, Jack; it's lying here in the snow in front of me. I don't know about the other two. But dude, we do have a swarm!"

Jack glanced at Dr. Lagarde, but he and Graham were fixated on the monitor. The images had changed: They were now a mosaic of moving video views of the rooftops and urban forest of Pasadena. Then the 210 Freeway was in sight. The swarm was almost home.

"Decelerate, please . . . ," Jack whispered. Suddenly the air was pierced by high-pitched whines, like the screams of miniature Stuka bombers.

An angry black swarm was swooping toward them at nearly Mach velocity. The "bats" were coming in at neck level with the obvious aim of decapitating Jack and his advisors.

"My god!" Dr. Graham threw his arms in front of his face as Dr. Lagarde hit the deck. But Jack just smiled.

As if in magical response to Jack's grin, the tiny bats abruptly cantered their wings and passed safely over the head of Dr. Graham.

Swwisshh! They decelerated and banked into a beautiful 360-degree turn over the eucalyptus trees and campus athletic fields. Circling around the library tower, they returned to the Guggenheim lab, hovering seven or eight feet above the roof.

Jack took a count. There were ten.

"Sebastian, we've lost another." He turned anxiously to Dr. Lagarde, who was trying to retrieve his badly shaken dignity.

"Don't worry about the casualties," Lagarde barked irritably. "Execute your program."

Jack typed something into his laptop.

Like a nervous hummingbird, one of the swarm slowly approached Dr. Graham. It leisurely circled his head, then hovered a few inches from his face. A glowing red dot in the bat's nose indicated that its tiny videocam was at work. The nearby monitor screen displayed every pore and whisker of the senior scientist's face.

The "microbat" was four inches long with a ten-inch wingspan, a little larger than the average dimensions of the local bats, *Antrozous pallidus*, that Jack and Sebastian had used for their airfoil design. Every evening thousands of the little yellow-brown pallid bats flutter out of the San Gabriel Mountains to hunt crickets, spiders, and even scorpions (they're uniquely immune to its sting) in the suburbs of Los Angeles.

One of the young engineers' key innovations was the versatility of the power sources for their microaerial vehicle (MAV). Instead of insects, their bats—whose bodies were both antennas and batteries—ate microwave energy transmitted from the ground; theoretically, this allowed them to stay aloft indefinitely within the range of microwave transmission (about ten miles).

Today's test, however, involved the addition of a pair of microjet engines—the size of AAA batteries—that had been first developed at Massachusetts Institute of Technology during the 1990s. These tiny engines operated at an incredible two million RPM and were capable of providing enough thrust to propel the bats at speeds in excess of two hundred MPH. Although the microjets ran out of fuel within three or four minutes, their booster power greatly extended the bats' capabilities.

Dr. Lagarde, who had doubted from the beginning whether Jack and Sebastian could design bat-shaped wings rigid enough for jet flight and flexible enough for hovering, was now a convert.

"Amazing," he cooed into the camera eye of the microbat.

"I agree," Dr. Graham added. "This may have significant application to planetary exploration. You young men are to be congratulated." He patted Jack on the back.

"OK, Jack," Lagarde resumed his usual crisp manner, "you and Sebastian put the bats back into their cave and meet me in my office at five."

As Lagarde turned to leave, the microbat followed him. "Jack, put that damn thing away!"

Jack laughed. "Sorry, Professor Lagarde, but it thought you were lonely." Lagarde gave a mock sneer.

Jack gently landed the swarm, then phoned Sebastian to put him out of his misery.

"Do you want the good news or bad news first?"

"Bad news?"

"Well, the good news is that we've won the Nobel Prize. The bad news is that one of our bats has a crush on Lagarde and tried to follow him home."

Sebastian giggled. "So the profs liked the swarm."

"Who wouldn't?" replied Jack. "They're adorable."

3. JACK'S SCRUPLES

Dr. Lagarde's office was at the far end of the microaerodynamics lab: a Santa's (or if you prefer, devil's) workshop of outlandish experimentation with miniaturized flying machines, some as small as bumblebees. Lagarde was world famous as the pioneer of the insectlike "entomopters" that NASA planned to use for its next Mars reconnaissance.

On the wall next to Lagarde's office was a Photoshop image concocted by one of his graduate students showing the Massachusetts Institute of Technology in flames as it was bombed by an armada of Caltech entomopters. The two schools were neck and neck (with Georgia Tech not far behind) in the high-stakes race to develop intelligent "swarms" of MAVs. This competition aroused deeper passions than college football.

The tiny flying machines were without a doubt the future of scientific reconnaissance, as well as the foundation for the Pentagon's dream of achieving battlefield omniscience. This greatly concerned Jack, who was as opposed to the military use of MAVs as he was excited by their scientific applications.

Dr. Lagarde cleared his throat.

"Here's the deal, guys. Sebastian, you are now officially a bug pilot, promoted to the NASA Mars entomopter project. My doctoral students will complain, but it will be character-building for them to have an undergraduate on the team. Congratulations."

Sebastian beamed from stem to stern as Lagarde shook his hand.

The professor then gave Jack a hard stare. "Hmmm . . . then there's you, Davis. I would love to have you aboard as well, but I know your qualms about working for the U.S. government . . ."

"On military research . . . sir," Jack corrected him. The Mars project had some DARPA as well as NASA funding, and he suspected the entomopters were actually military technology in disguise. He had extracted a promise from Sebastian that none of their microbat research would be shared with Pentagon types.

Lagarde sighed. It was fruitless arguing with Jack about his deeply held aversions to war and nationalism.

"OK, Mr. Peacenik. With the permission of the Dean of Engineering, I am granting you a semester's field leave—officially, this is an independent research project. You are authorized to take the microwave and laser gear with you, as well as the bats and their paraphernalia. This stuff is all insured, but you aren't. Understand?"

Jack nodded.

"So if you fall into a sinkhole or get abducted by Somali pirates, Caltech is not responsible. I've written official letters of introduction to smooth the way with the Yemeni government, but don't expect the university to ride to your rescue under any circumstance. And given your anarchist attitudes, don't count on Washington or Dublin raising a sweat on your behalf either. So please—stay out of trouble."

Jack—born in Los Angeles but raised in Dublin—had dual U.S. and Irish citizenship, but he considered himself an "internationalist" in the hallowed tradition of the scientists he most admired: Cuvier, Wallace, Kropotkin, Fermi, Pauling, and Gould.

"Don't worry, Professor, I'm in the hands of a good crew."

Dr. Lagarde squinted hard at Jack. "I am not sure that's entirely true, young man. Your record shows that you were a participant in a rather tragic episode in Greenland, along with your brother and several friends."

"Oh . . . " Jack was taken aback for a second. "We've all learned our lessons. We're older and more responsible now."

"I hope so," said Lagarde. "Well, at any event, your proposal for using MAVs to explore cave ecosystems is exciting science, so I'm going to root for you. And . . . oh yes . . . I have a small going-away present."

Lagarde pushed a small titanium box across the table. "Open it."

There was a glass tube inside the box, and it appeared to contain flakes of gold. Jack's jaw dropped, and Sebastian's eyes popped out.

"E-dust!"

"Yes indeed. Since you have the rest of the necessary equipment, I thought you might have fun experimenting with some of Caltech's finest vintage E-dust. But just remember, except under a microscope, this looks very similar to the Pentagon variety, so don't get into trouble. I've enclosed documentation to prove that it's unclassified and doesn't violate the Patriot Act or any other laws."

"Thanks, Dr. Lagarde, this will help a lot. I'll send you weekly field reports as soon as we arrive at the research station."

"Well then. Good luck." Student and professor shook hands.

Jack and Sebastian grinned at each other. After long months as scientific hermits, it was time to celebrate with the gang.

4. FEMTOCHEMISTRY

Their hangout was Lucky Baldwin's Pub in Old Town Pasadena, half a mile from campus. In addition to the myriad brews on tap, it had a nice selection of Irish tunes on the jukebox for those occasions—more frequent these days—when Jack was homesick.

A dozen or so of their mates were gathered around a large patio table. The centerpiece, rising above innumerable pints of stout, was the dead bat from Mt. Wilson carefully interred in a mock coffin that Sebastian had fabricated from a shoebox.

Earlier in the development of the project, Jack and Sebastian had taken turns giving all the bats Chinese and Irish names.

"Goodbye, Wu Lin, loyal servant . . ."

"Naw, Sebastian, that's not Wu Lin." Jack was a bit lubricated, but less so than Sebastian.

"What do you mean, not Wu Lin? Which one is it then?" Sebastian pretended to be shocked.

"I think its Seamus," Jack snorted.

"Ah, maybe so," conceded Sebastian. "The Irish bats don't fly as well as the Chinese. They get drunk and fall on their faces."

The crowd laughed, Jack the loudest.

"So, Jack, tell me about this mysterious adventure you're embarking on."

It was Sebastian's cousin Lucy, a senior in physical chemistry. Her real major, however, was impersonating Marlene Dietrich and Mata Hari. Her dark eyes were hooded with worldliness, and she held a cigarette in a long antique silver holder.

"Lucy, do all Hong Kong girls act like central European *femmes fatales*?"

"Only those from the femtochemistry lab. So little time and so many reactions."

Lucy worked in Nobel laureate Ahmed Zewail's lab analyzing chemical reactions at "femto" time scales: one millionth of a billionth of a second.

Jack chuckled. "OK, Lucy, I'll tell you all my dark secrets." (Jack's real secret was that he fancied Lucy but had never had the nerve to ask her for a date.)

"My brother and I have been invited to join a UN scientific team doing cave ecology on the island of Socotra. As you probably know, Socotra is often called the 'Galapagos of the Indian Ocean' because of its extraordinary native fauna and flora. The UN is in the final stages of negotiations with the government of Yemen, which administers Socotra, to declare the island a World Heritage site. The missing link in the scientific documentation of its biodiversity is a serious reconnaissance of its biological underworld."

"Big mysterious caves full of sinister eyeless monsters . . ." Lucy blew a smoke ring around Jack's nose; it tickled.

"Lucy, you're such a romantic. But no one really knows what's under Socotra. A few years ago Belgian speleologists briefly explored some of the better-known caves and found several new species, so we're quite excited by what we might discover in a full field season."

"But why you and your brother? Conor, as I recall, is the wonderboy of Ice Age megafauna, and you're a MAV geek."

Jack was on the defensive. "Well, Conor's advisor thinks he needs a vacation from the Pleistocene, and Sebastian and I designed the microbats with cave exploration as part of the mission."

"I see." Lucy crossed her legs. She enjoyed interrogating the handsome Irish boy who was usually too preoccupied with bats to be part of the Caltech social scene. "So how about your love interest on this expedition. Is that 'science' too?"

Jack blushed. "No . . . Julia—Julia Monk is her name—is our old friend. She was with us in Greenland four years ago. She's a wildlife biologist. Her advisor at Columbia, Dr. Hasan, is the head of the team."

"Jack, don't be embarrassed. I was just teasing."

"Sorry, Lucy, guess I've become a bit of a wallflower."

"Well, come back in May and we'll see if we can do something about that." She blew a kiss as she traded places with Sebastian.

"My cousin giving you a hard time again?"

"She makes me stutter."

"Well, that's because you're just a hick from Dublin. I need to give you some pointers on urban sophistication."

"You Hong Kong types are as bad as New Yorkers."

"Worse." Sebastian grinned, then became serious. "Jack, what's the real deal with this Socotra trip?"

"What do you mean?"

"Look, I'm your best friend, so don't hide anything from me. I know you and your brother were involved in some kind of secret goings-on in the Arctic a few years back. And now you're headed off to this enigmatic pirate island, exploring caves that are probably the underground headquarters of al-Qaeda."

"No, Ali Baba and the Forty Thieves," Jack interrupted.

"Be serious, Jack. This cave stuff sounds like a cover story. And why did Dr. Lagarde give you the E-dust? Are you working for the CIA? The Defense Intelligence Agency? The Irish whatever-it's-called? Come on, tell me, I can keep a secret."

"Sebastian, you know I hate all that covert science, James Bond stuff. This is just ordinary UN-sponsored fieldwork. I won't be jumping from rock to rock with a cutlass between my teeth."

"Are you sure?"

"Absolutely."

"Well, I suppose you are on the level." Sebastian came closer and whispered. "But if anything dangerous does come up, if you get into any kind of tight situation, call your Caltech brother. Me and my Hong Kong homeboys can be there in twenty-four hours. Promise."

Jack was touched by this gesture from his bighearted but now thoroughly inebriated bat pal.

"OK, Sebastian," he whispered back conspiratorially, "I'm counting on you."

Sebastian was now content. After a long round of handshakes, hugs, and a final wink to Lucy Chen, Jack walked home to his dorm. In the palm trees there was the telltale flutter he had come to know so well: hungry little pallid bats.

5. HIROSHIMA

Jack spent the next morning and most of the afternoon at Los Angeles International Airport completing the paperwork and inspections needed to get his bats and scientific gear aboard Aer Lingus to Dublin. When he finally stumbled into the departure lounge, he was only in the mood for imaginative relaxation, so he cracked open a new novel by his favorite sci-fi writer, Octavia Butler. Somehow he ignored the headlines screaming from every news rack in the airport:

HIROSHIMA-LIKE EXPLOSION DETECTED BY SATELLITES

JAPANESE TANKER MISSING

SUPER-TERRORISTS STRIKE AGAIN

(AP: Djibouti) U.S. military satellites have detected an enormous fireball in the Indian Ocean, near the east end of the island of Socotra, a dependency of Yemen. Shipping in the vicinity also reports a huge explosion and horizon on fire. Although apparently no SOS signals were received, Gyco Oil Corporation, based in Yokohoma, says that one of its tankers, carrying highly flammable aviation fuel, is missing.

Antiterrorism experts speculate that the ship may have been target of al-Qaeda or possibly Somali warlords. Local pirates are considered incapable of such destruction. The experts warn this may be beginning of full-scale attack on Red Sea and Indian Ocean commerce.

The huge explosion has set off military alarms around the world. U.S. military aircraft and a nuclear submarine are reportedly already on the scene. Several supertankers have been diverted to a safe haven at Bahrain, and India and Australia have sent out long-range aircraft to protect shipping. Tokyo newspapers report the government is considering dispatching missile frigates to Diego Garcia and the Strait of Malacca.

In light of the potential threat to the world oil supply, the Group of Seven has scheduled an emergency meeting of foreign ministers. The Arab League also plans to meet. The U.S. Homeland Security czar may declare a code red national alert.

CHAPTER TWO: *Invitation to an Island*

. . . it is called Dioscorida, and is very large but desert and marshy, having rivers in it and crocodiles and many snakes and great lizards, of which the flesh is eaten and the fat melted and used instead of olive oil. The island yields no fruit, neither vine nor grain. The inhabitants are few and they live on the coast toward the north, which from this side faces the continent. They are foreigners, a mixture of Arabs and Indians and Greeks, who have emigrated to carry on trade there.

SOCOTRA DESCRIBED IN *The Periplus of the Erythraean Sea*[5]

6. CONOR'S GRAY HAIR

Jack's brother Conor was waiting to help him clear his scientific gear through customs at Dublin Airport. It had been almost half a year since his last homecoming.

"Ya big plonker," Conor kidded. "Ya *culchie.*"

"Ya muzzy," Jack rejoined.

"I missed you, big brother."

"Missed you too."

They gave each other a long bear hug.

"So what do you think of the apocalypse off Socotra?"

"Huh?" Jack was fatigued from the ten-hour flight.

"Don't you gooney birds in Lotusland ever read a paper?"

"I've honestly been too busy with my honors project."

Conor showed him the morning headlines in the *Irish Times.*

Jack was stunned; he felt sympathy for the families of the lost crew. "Do you think this will nix our plans?" he asked Conor.

"No, not at all. Our UN liaison in San'a phoned to say that everything is going ahead, but the government is sending lots of troops to the island. Possibly Yanks as well. Our real problem is Mom: she's pretty distressed by all the coverage about pirates and terrorists. For weeks I've been reassuring her that Socotra is a quiet garden spot, so I need your help calming her down. After all, you're the family's paragon of responsibility."

Jack nodded wearily. He was inured to the tedious burden of "responsibility." Then he suddenly noticed that Conor was gray on one side of his head.

"Have you prematurely aged? Nineteen years old with gray hair?"

Conor giggled. "Not gray, singed. Paddy Mullen and I were involved in a wee lab explosion."

"Lab explosion? My God, Conor, what have you been up to this time?"

"Just testing a smidgen of C-4. We miscalculated and blew up the Nissen shack we were using for a lab."

"C-4? Are you daft? You're a paleontologist. What are you fooling around plastique explosives for? Have you joined the IRA?"

Conor loved it when Jack got riled—it was just like the old days.

"Calm down, the Irish Army lent it to us. We're trying to figure out how to excavate permafrost. Most mammoth or mastodon remains are recovered during the spring melt and instantly attacked by bacteria. If we're going to get good DNA we need to work in the winter, and that means we have to gently blow up some terrain."

"Gently blow up some terrain?" Jack was incredulous.

7. JULIA'S LETTER

The next morning the newspaper—(which Jack read, for a change)—revealed that the crew of the *Ryukyu Rainbow*, who had managed to abandon ship before the inferno, had been rescued by a passing bulk carrier. The captain told his rescuers that local pirates had unintentionally destroyed the ship's automatic steering and navigation systems. The international crisis around Socotra de-escalated, and there was no red alert in America after all.

Meanwhile, Jack's two days in Dublin passed softly in the bosom of his family and in reunions with his host of cousins and former schoolmates. He had been greatly missed by those at home.

Despite Conor's dangerous new hobby, Jack was impressed with how grown-up his wild Irish rogue of a little brother had become. Although three years younger than Jack, Conor was already a published authority on mammoths and the second-youngest doctoral student in the history of UCD; he had even narrated a documentary about the Ice Age for Irish television.

Conor had also become a passionate environmental activist. His best friend Qav—the young Inuit biologist who had shared their extraordinary adventures four years ago—was now running the premier wildlife research station in the Arctic. Using the Internet, the two of them had started a campaign for the biodiversity hot spot of southeast Greenland to be designated a World Heritage site, like the Galapagos, and soon, Socotra.

"Conor, I'm really going to miss Qav on this expedition."

"I know, Julia said the same thing. But since his grandfather developed arthritis, the whole logistical burden of supporting Dr. Dansgaard has fallen on Qav. I'm hoping to visit him in August."

"Provided we survive Socotra."

"What do you mean?"

"I dunno, I just have a bad premonition that we're about to fall into another crevasse full of danger and intrigue. You know my mate Sebastian at Caltech actually suspects that we are secret agents working for the CIA or something."

"Of course we are, except we're hit men for the World Wildlife Fund." Conor giggled.

"No, seriously Conor, don't you have any apprehensions?"

"Well, my worry has been the opposite: that we would find no mystery in Socotra at all, except for maybe a few blind crickets or albino spiders in a cave. But then I received a letter from Julia a few days ago that has me really jazzed. Here, you read it."

Hadibo, Socotra
January 24

Dear Conor,

First of all, discard your propaganda goggles about the Arab world and pirates. This is a wonderful culture—extremely poor and frugal but also generous, kindhearted, and courageous. You will marvel at how a Bedouin society has adapted itself to life on an isolated island, and the extraordinary attention they have given to sustainable resource management. Although the position of women leaves much to be desired, it is more egalitarian than on the mainland. And—good news for your anarchist older brother—there is still little state apparatus here: the Yemenis tread gingerly on the Socotris' traditions of self-government. This could change, of course, in face of the coming tidal wave of ecotourism, or if the island is tragically annexed to the regional conflicts raging around it. But for the moment, this is a place of hope, like Chiapas or Nunavut.

Secondly, we have the world's best team leader. As you know, at the last moment I chose Columbia over Caltech because of the Biosphere in Arizona, which Columbia manages. That's where I met Dr. Hasan. He grew up in a

Palestinian refugee camp and was a public-health doctor in Gaza before getting his PhD in biogeochemistry. It was his idea to develop an environmental management plan before Socotra's caves were overrun with foreign spelunkers. The underground water resources are especially valuable to the Socotris.

You'll love Dr. Hasan's family. His wife Samira is a pediatrician from Brooklyn and my best chum. They have an adorable toddler, Omar, who already speaks three languages (English, Arabic, and some Socotri). Omar and I share a pet civet called Weasel, the most fearless cave explorer on the island.

OK, now I am really going to light a fire under your seat. The third piece of good news is that the karst cave ecology here is immense. The friendly Belgian speleologists were back this fall, and they now believe that the major caves are interconnected: something like Mammoth Caves in the USA. There could be sixty miles or more of passages, chambers, and underground rivers.

But every Labryinth needs its Minotaur. So, fourthly, we have MYSTERY here, in capital letters. Big time. The locals believe that dragons live under the island! Goats, even children, disappear; monstrous footprints are found; pale giant shapes are glimpsed in the mouth of caves, and so on. That's why they are so reluctant to venture very deeply into the caves.

Superstition? I don't think so. Check out the section on Socotra (or "Dioscorida," as it was called by the Greeks) in The Periplus of the Erythraean Sea. Classical scholars think this first-century A.D. navigation guide to the Indian Ocean is fairly accurate. The author makes a big deal about Socotra's crocodiles and the "great lizards" that provided the locals' staple diet. When and how did they become extinct? Or could they have gone underground and survived? Or maybe—and this is my favorite hypothesis—"lizard" is a misnomer; ecologically, giant salamanders would be more likely.

Are you salivating? Hope so. This marvelous island is one of the last great terrestrial frontiers for evolutionary biology. But we have to work quickly. The Socotri are in a race against time to preserve their culture and natural habitats. The heavy lug-soled boots of "ecotourism" (I hate that term) will be here in the near future. So you and Jack get here sooner. Pronto.

I'll greatly miss Qav, but we can still be the Three Musketeers, even if our D'Artagnan is in Greenland.

Love,

Julia

Jack and Conor had a long slog to join up with Julia: from Dublin they flew to London to catch the weekly flight to San'a, with a stopover in Rome. They had to arrive hours early at Gatwick to oversee the transfer of their half-ton of baggage: all of Jack's Caltech equipment, plus Conor's climbing gear and sea kayak.

At last, after a long day of filling out customs forms and having their baggage x-rayed, they were in the air. London to San'a was a ten-hour flight, so they curled up with a couple of good books.

"What are you reading, Jack? One of your anarchist tracts?"

"Well, in a way it is. This is the British explorer Wellsted's account of the two months that he spent on Socotra in the summer of 1834. He is talking about the indigenous Socotri, the pastoral people who have lived in the mountains for millennia. Can I read you an extract?"

"Sure."

There were no sheikhs nor governor; every one pursues uninterruptedly his own avocations . . . [and] notwithstanding the singular anomaly of so great a number of people residing together without any chiefs or laws, offenses against the good order appear infinitely less frequent than among the more civilized nations. Theft, murder, and other heinous crimes are almost unknown.[6]

"Oh, I get it," laughed Conor. "You think Socotra used to be a utopia where everyone simply raised goats, minded their own business, and loved their neighbor."

"Don't be so cynical, Conor," Jack scolded. "Almost all travelers' accounts attest to the Socotris' success at social self-organization without violence, jails, or rulers. It confirms Kropotkin's theories."

"Prince Peter Kropotkin, the nineteenth-century anarchist?"

"Yes, but remember that he was also a great scientist. Based on his fieldwork in Siberia, he showed that cooperation was as fundamental in natural history as competition—Socotra is just more proof of the power of mutual aid without coercion."

Jack realized that he was beginning to sound preachy, so he changed the subject.

"How 'bout you? What you reading?"

Conor was deep into a huge volume with a brown-paper bookcover that hid the title.

"Take a look."

"The *Dow Blaster's Handbook.*" Jack suddenly felt clammy, even nauseous. "Are you out of your mind?" he whispered fiercely. "You're toting an encyclopedia of explosives around the Middle East?"

Conor smiled serenely. "Calm down, Jack. I'm merely interested in blowing up permafrost."

But his older brother could just envision the dungeon that undoubtedly awaited them in Yemen.

9. SINISTER SUNGLASSES

However, it was Jack's bats, not Conor's bookbag, that got them in trouble.

After landing at San'a, all their gear was transferred to a special shed, where it was inspected by several customs agents and a Yemeni military intelligence officer named Ali. An avuncular Dutchman, Gert Harmsen, represented the United Nations Development Programme, the official sponsor of the Socotra expedition.

Captain Ali spoke fluent English with a bizarre Texas accent. A connoisseur of high-tech gear, he lavishly praised Conor for his superb selection of climbing and spelunking equipment, but he was particularly struck by the sleek little watercraft. No one in Arabia, of course, had seen a Greenlandic kayak before, and Ali was incredulous when Conor described its acrobatic capabilities in a rough sea. As a souvenir, he insisted on taking a snapshot of Conor pretending to paddle the kayak.

All seemed to be going splendidly until it was Jack's turn. The captain instantly became less friendly when Jack explained that his crates contained a state-of-the-art microaerial reconnaissance system. Although Mr. Harmsen reminded the captain that the UN had already submitted proper customs declarations, including a complete technical description of the Caltech gear, Ali remained stubbornly suspicious.

"This is spy equipment, no? Only the Pentagon has threshold technology like this. And these so-called 'bats' of yours aren't for cave exploration. They are obviously for surveillance of some kind."

Jack argued fruitlessly with Captain Ali.

"Just wait here, young Mr. James Bond," Ali finally ordered. He went to the far end of the shed and called someone on a cell phone; he still seemed to be speaking English to whoever was on the other end.

Five minutes later, Conor looked out the window and saw a desert-camouflaged military Humvee approaching. There was an M-16 sticking out of one window.

"Ooh, Jack, I think they're going to throw us in the slammer."

Jack and Conor exchanged grim looks.

There were several figures in the Humvee, but only one got out. He was a tall, blond, muscular white man wearing a Hawaiian shirt, blue jeans, and combat boots. Wraparound Ray-Ban sunglasses gave him a decidedly sinister look.

Ali met him at the door, and they conferred excitedly for a few minutes; then the newcomer came toward Jack.

"OK, partner, open the crates." It was another Texas accent.

Jack stood his ground. "Excuse me, but who are you? This scientific equipment is consigned to the United Nations and has been properly documented and approved for transit to Socotra."

"I said, open those crates," said the sunglasses, in a truly menacing drawl.

Jack looked at Harmsen. "Go ahead, Jack, do what he says."

For the next half hour, Ali and the mysterious Yank minutely studied Jack's gear. They took dozens of Polaroid photographs. To allay their paranoia, Jack offered them a copy of his Caltech research proposal; it was accepted without a thank-you.

The American then took Ali off into a corner. He seemed to be giving his Yemeni subordinate instructions, and Ali nodded obligingly. Finally, the American shot a poisonous look at Jack and Conor, wheeled about-face with military precision, and left. The Humvee fishtailed away from the customs shed in a trailing cloud of sand.

Captain Ali was now friendlier. "Well, we've finally sorted out the confusion, and you are now free to transport this equipment to Socotra."

The boys smiled in relief.

"Oh, but one small detail," Captain Ali sighed.

"What's that?" Jack asked anxiously.

"We'll have to keep one of your little 'bats' here in quarantine. Bats have distemper and sometimes carry rabies, you know." Ali laughed cruelly. "Perhaps you can have it back when you leave Yemen in April."

Jack was incensed: he realized that the only reason to "quarantine" his bat was to allow the Americans to study its construction and operation. So much for his elaborate efforts to keep his research out of the hands of the Pentagon.

Jack wanted to protest, but Harmsen whispered in his ear: "Give in, Jack. There's nothing we can do."

"OK, Captain Ali, take your pick," Jack said bitterly.

"*Il-Hamdu li-Ilah,*" Ali thanked him in Arabic. "Your equipment will be transferred to the UN hangar for your flight tomorrow afternoon. "*Ma'a s-salama.*"

Ali cradled his captive microbat like a newborn baby. Jack wondered how he would explain to Sebastian that "Mao" had been kidnapped.

10. GOLD DUST

Gert Harmsen tried to calm the brothers down. He explained that since the explosion of the *Ryukyu Rainbow*, U.S. elite units were swarming all over the Gulf of Aden region. American fears, as usual, might be exaggerated, but the UN's *modus operandi* was to cut Washington as much slack as possible. That's why, he explained apologetically, there would be no formal complaint about the theft of Jack's bat. Harmsen ordered the boys a cab and promised to stop by their hotel first thing in the morning.

Conor and Jack were still too upset to pay any attention to the picturesque scenery between the airport and Yemen's capital.

"Who was that mean mugger in the shades?" asked Conor.

"Take your pick: CIA, DIA, Delta Force, Special Forces . . ."

"Well, Mr. Schwarzenegger had Ali jumping like a puppet on a string. Do the bloody Yanks own this country?"

"No, I don't think so. But since al-Qaeda blew up the USS *Cole* in Aden Harbor a few years back, they've maintained huge pressure on Yemen. I suppose the locals feel they have to bend over backwards to reassure Washington that they aren't sheltering terrorists."

"But why are they so interested in your bats?"

"Well, as you'll see in a few days, the wings can morph from one state to another. I don't think the Pentagon has MAVs that can do that yet. I've been under a lot of pressure at Caltech to share the design with senior researchers who have Pentagon ties. Fortunately, Sebastian, although he has different political views, has agreed to keep the bats out of uniform."

"Any chance this was all a setup? A comedy planned long in advance?"

"Why not? Since I won't give them the design, they simply steal it. And they stage the stunt so that it looks like a spur-of-the-moment decision."

"And the UN rolls over . . ." Conor was disgusted at Harmsen's meekness.

"Yeah. But at least they didn't search us."

Conor was puzzled. "Why, what would they find? Are you carrying something?"

Jack reached into his pocket and pulled out a glass vial filled with golden grains. He handed it to his brother.

Conor carefully examined it. "What the heck is this stuff?"

"Magic dust right out of the *Arabian Nights*. I'll show you what it does when we get to Socotra."

11. FRIENDLY COINCIDENCE

Their destination was Hotel Taj Talha next to the famous Qubbat at-Talha mosque in Old San'a. As their cab threaded its way through the clamoring congestion of the *medina*, Jack and Conor were struck with wonder.

"Incredible—it looks like a Muslim Florence," gushed Jack.

"Or maybe medieval Manhattan," suggested Conor.

Most of the architecture of the old city was actually contemporary with Shakespeare's London, although some was much older. The Great Mosque, for instance, had been constructed during the lifetime of Prophet Mohammed himself. The only modern elements in Old San'a were the satellite dishes on the rooftops and the holes punched in the *medina* walls to allow the invasion of honking automobiles and cabs.

Whole clans and extended families lived in extraordinary tower houses constructed of basalt stone and sun-dried brick which soared up to a hundred feet above the cobbled streets and crooked lanes. Their brightly colored stained-glass windows were framed within bold geometries and zigzag puzzles of white gypsum. The swollen domes of mosques and bullet-shaped spires of minarets added to the magical syncopation of the skyline.

Jack rolled down the cab window. "Wow, this is sensory overload."

The din competed with the smell.

"I'm going to try an experiment," Conor shouted. He held his nose and closed his eyes. His ears exploded with a crazy sympathy of motorcycles backfiring, donkeys braying, street singers crooning, *muezzins* calling the faithful to prayer, cassettes blasting Egyptian pop tunes, and what sounded ominously like automatic weapon fire.

"Incredible. OK, now I am going to close my eyes and hold my hands over my ears. You do the same." Jack complied, and the boys' nostrils were immediately invaded by a maelstrom of fragrance and stink: ripe fruit, car exhaust, garlic, donkey manure, musky perfumes, pungent cheeses, saddle leather, roasting coffee, sweat, and *qat* smoke (*qat* is the mild narcotic that is the basis of male social life in Yemen).

"I never knew smell could be so psychedelic," laughed Jack. "San'a is overwhelming . . ."

"I'm game to go out exploring, how 'bout you?" replied Conor.

"Absolutely." The brothers had temporarily forgotten both anger and jet lag.

Their cab pulled up in front of the hotel; Jack apologized for paying in dollars, but their driver was delighted. The boys quickly stowed their bags in their room, and following the advice of the desk clerk, exchanged some euros and dollars for local *riyals*.

On the street they were immediately self-conscious about their casual Western dress.

"I feel like I'm wearing a sign," complained Conor.

"Well, I'm afraid we're going to have to get used to being curiosities. I mean, look at you." Jack pointed to his brother's light-blue eyes and straw-colored hair. "Conor of Arabia."

They were standing in front of the at-Talha mosque when a bespectacled young man in a loose gown emerged from behind a column.

"*Min wayn intkum? Min Amrika?*" he demanded angrily.

Conor had managed to cram in a little Arabic over the past few weeks. "*La. Ihna min Irelanda. Titkallam inglizi?*" he replied calmly.

"Yes, I speak English." The man's voice softened. "In fact, I've been to Dublin. Are you from there?"

"Born and bred. I'm studying at University College. Quaternary science."

"UCD?" Their interrogator was suddenly ecstatic. "Why, I was exchange student for year at UCD. Electrical engineering . . . my name is Muhammad Qa'id al-Husayni." He extended his hand with a broad smile.

"I'm Conor, and this is my big brother Jack." They clasped Muhammad's hand warmly.

"Surely this must be miracle. UCD reunion here in front of mosque."

"Certainly I think so," Jack spoke up for the first time. "Do you realize, Muhammed, you're only the fourth or fifth person we've met in this country. What a coincidence!"

"No coincidence, my friends. Fate has brought us together. Now, let me take you to a meal. I apologize that I cannot invite you to my home for feast, but I'm only visiting. I am from al-Mukallah, far away on the east coast. I hope you're hungry."

"Aye, famished. I could eat a baby's arse through the bars of a cot," replied Conor.

Jack slugged Conor on the shoulder.

"What did he just say?" puzzled Muhammed, whose time in Dublin had been too brief to acquire a mastery of street argot.

"He said thanks, we'd love to join you for a meal."

Muhammed expertly shepherded them through a delirious maze of alleys and *suqs* (markets) until they arrived at Ali's Restaurant.

"Oh my god, I've read about this," Conor whispered to his brother. "In Mackintosh-Smith's book—this joint is legendary. Top of the line."

As indeed it was. Muhammed chuckled with delight as his new friends lustily savored their first fiery bowls of *saltah* topped with *hulbah*, followed by sweet tea, figs, and honey. In the back of the restaurant someone was plucking a plangent tune on an *oud*.

"Wow, this is like eating hot coals." Conor perspired as he soaked up the last of the chili-saturated lamb and garlic stew with a piece of golden-brown *mulouj*.

Before Jack could speak he had to quench the wildfire in his throat with half a gallon of cold water. He smiled at Muhammed.

"You were really angry when you thought we were Americans, weren't you?"

Muhammed sighed and explained that he had nothing against ordinary American tourists. God knows, tens of thousands of Yemenis had immigrated to the States; he himself had a cousin near Detroit.

On the other hand, he hated the swaggering way that some Yanks—obviously CIA or Special Forces—moved around his country giving orders to one and all and occasionally assassinating the odd local "terrorist" with their sinister Hellfire missiles.

Conor gave Jack a long look. "Tell Muhammed what happened to us this afternoon. Tell him about our friend with the shades."

Jack rehearsed the background of their visit to Yemen. He told Muhammed about their research, their excitement about Socotra, their strange encounter at the airport, and the theft of his bat. Muhammed listened intently.

"You must be very cautious, my good friends. Nothing in the world these days is as it seems. A few months ago, I would have said yes, by all means, do your project in Socotra. But now I don't know. I thank you for helping my country, but I must warn you—there is danger."

"What do you mean?" Conor sensed that Muhammed knew more than he was saying.

"Look, I am from al-Mukallah on the coast. My brothers are sailors and traders, yes? Recently very strange things go on. Something big is brewing. Maybe a war, maybe al-Qaeda, maybe spaceships land. Who knows?" He laughed, then became serious again. "But it is important that you take care and trust no one."

"Is all this because of the tanker that was pirated and blew up?" Jack asked.

"No, tensions were already high months before. My brothers see lots of strange things at sea. Very scared."

"Is Socotra involved?" It was Conor's turn.

Muhammed's face changed into that expression that doctors wear when they're about to tell a patient he has an incurable disease.

"Socotra maybe the center of all this. I think Socotra is big mystery, and . . ." he paused, "very deadly place to be at wrong time. Americans think bin Laden is hiding there. But what you really must fear—more than anything—is al-Kaitos."

"Kaitos?"

"Yes, 'The Whale.' He is Socotri pirate with a monstrous, deformed body. Every trader, pilgrim, and fisherman in the Gulf of Aden—completely terrified of him. He lurks off the coast of Socotra. Beware Kaitos."

Muhammed realized that he had sent a chill up his two friends' backs.

"Look, I'm sorry. I don't want to scare you. Let me give you the call letters for my brothers' boat. I will see them soon and explain that you are my friends. If you have shortwave radio, you can always reach them. In any emergency, they will help you. They know the waters around Socotra like you know pubs on O'Connell Street."

Jack and Conor laughed.

"Listen, we appreciate you looking out for us. And we'll certainly take your advice to heart." Conor was delighted that they had already made a friend, even if he was the bearer of strange warnings.

The Yemeni UCD alumnus escorted his friends back to their hotel and gave them a traditional embrace in parting. Under his breath he also said an anxious prayer for their survival.

CHAPTER THREE: *The Cave People*

I have travelled much amidst the mountain scenery of Arabia, of Persia, and of India; but that of Socotra, in wildness and romantic grandeur, surpasses them all.

LT. J. R. WELLSTED (1840)[7]

12. FASTBALL

Julia at last.

The same thought was in both brothers' minds as their small prop jet broke through the low-lying clouds over the north coast of Socotra. From the port window they could see the whitecaps on the Indian Ocean, then sand dunes, mangrove swamps, and a navigation beacon. A few seconds later, the plane's wheels slapped hard against the tarmac of the runway.

The airport was only a few years old, the first installment in a new infrastructure designed to open up Socotra and its 40,000 or so inhabitants to the modern world. A group of workers was still putting stucco on the sides of the attractive little terminal building, while others planted young date palms in front of the entrance.

The military part of the airport was several hundreds yards away, behind a formidable revetment of sandbags and razor wire. A Yemeni fighter jet, probably a MiG-21, was parked next to two Black Hawk helicopters with American insignia. Yemeni Special Forces soldiers in red berets stood guard.

Meanwhile, the pilot shut down his engines and cranked down the stairs. Several local UN employees were already waiting with a flatbed truck to help Jack and Conor unload their equipment. The day was overcast but pleasantly warm, reminiscent of Dublin in June.

"Where's our Julia?" Conor asked anxiously.

"There, I think," Jack pointed to two Land Rovers headed toward them. As the vehicles came closer, they could see the mud-splattered blue UN symbols on the sides.

Julia emerged wearing a khaki suit and dark glasses; she was carrying Weasel, her cave-exploring pet civet. Her brown hair was bobbed short, and she seemed much taller than either boy had remembered. Both were suddenly self-conscious about their own modest stature.

"Well, well, Weasel, look what the monsoon has brought to town. Batman and Mammoth Boy."

She gave each of them a warm hug and peck on the cheek. She had expected Jack to be a bit shy—as always—but was surprised when Conor blushed as well.

"Hiya," Conor managed.

Julia gestured to the group of people who had arrived with her. "OK, let me do the introductions. This is my fellow New Yorker, Samira—she runs the island's Well Baby project. And this is her own adorable baby, Omar."

Samira, also in khaki and wearing a scarf, was even taller than Julia, with a broad smile, gorgeous black sparkling eyes, and a no-nonsense Brooklyn handshake. When Conor bent down to get closer to Omar, the vivacious toddler jumped into his arms and stayed there. Conor was delighted.

"And this is Anwar, our administrator. He manages finance, logistics, and government relations. Tariq and Hadad run the motor pool, which, in Socotra, means they're sorcerers and pirates."

Julia repeated the last phrase in Arabic, and Tariq and Hadad, handsome young Socotris who had learned car repair while working in Saudi Arabia, nodded approvingly. Anwar, an older mainlander with a gentle face and distinguished gray beard, shook his head in mock disapproval.

"And finally, meet your boss, and mine, Dr. Hasan."

Hasan was a short, wiry man of forty in Levis and a New York Mets sweatshirt. He had a slight limp from an old shrapnel wound received when he was working as a young doctor in Gaza. A fanatical baseball fan, he had already distributed enough ancient mitts and hardballs to form Socotra's first Little League team, and he was currently experimenting with making super-performance baseball bats out of exotic local woods.

"What position do you guys play?" It was not the first question that Jack and Conor had expected from their senior scientist.

"Um, what sport?" Jack hesitantly inquired.

"Baseball, of course!" Hasan boomed.

"My dad took me to a game once," Jack fumbled. "I thought the physics was interesting, but the play was rather slow."

Hasan glared at him and then turned to Conor. "And you, mister?"

"Me brother's right." Conor's eyes twinkled as he torqued up his accent. "Baseball is almost as exciting as waiting in the dentist's office.

Now, if it's action you like, try a wee bit of the *sliotar*."

Dr. Hasan narrowed his eyes. "Come again?"

"Hurling, Professor, our Gaelic crown jewel and the fastest field sport on earth. A sharp slice of the *bas*, and the *sliotar* is traveling at the speed of light. I'm a forward on the UCD geology team. We're the terrors of the Irish earth sciences. Of course, we're often in 'dissent' and I've been 'booked' a few times meself . . ."

Julia was laughing. "Now *this* is the Conor I remember."

"Indeed," added Jack. "Blarney cubed and divided by the square root of negative two."

"Well, Conor." Now Hasan's eyes were twinkling. "I accept this as a challenge. My fastball versus your warp-speed '*sliotar*.' But first, let's go home and eat."

Hasan slapped Conor on the back, and Julia gave Jack another hug. The expedition climbed into their Land Rovers and set off in the direction of the great brooding spires of the Hajhir Mountains.

13. JULIA'S NEW BABY

Socotra's only paved road connected the new airport to the island's dusty little capital of Hadibo. From there a dirt—or rather mud—road followed a *wadi* (wash) past date plantations and a few slumbering camels into the mouth of a rocky canyon deeply incised into the Hajhir. A rocky, bone-shattering track then climbed steeply to a small plateau with a perennial creek where Samira's pediatric clinic shared a mud-walled compound with the UN's Speleobiology Project.

Conor rode with Dr. Hasan and Anwar, Omar still on his lap and his kayak strapped to the roof, while Jack shared the other Land Rover with Samira and Julia. Tariq and Hadad followed behind with the rest of the gear in the beat-up truck.

"Here, give Weasel a cuddle." Julie dropped the civet on Jack's lap.

Weasel—a lesser Indian civet cat (*Viverricula indica*)—was sleek like a mongoose but bigger, nearly the size of a racoon. The fluffy fur on his chest was spotted, but the rest of his body was striped and his tail was ringed. He had a small, handsome head with intelligent but wicked eyes.

His claws looked razor sharp, and when Jack stroked him he opened his mouth to expose equally vicious-looking teeth. On an island which had never known dogs, he was top carnivore.

"What does he eat?"

"Goat meat, rats, feral cats, and anyone who displeases him."

Jack, nervously cradling Weasel, recalled a description of Socotran civets by an Oxford expedition in the 1950s: "All teeth and claws and growl and stink."

"I didn't think you could domesticate civets. I mean, these are very aggressive animals, kind of like tropical wolverines, right?"

"Sure, a civet can lick animals three times their size. Right, Weasel?"

Julia's civet hissed in agreement and again showed his teeth.

"So how did you tame him?"

"With love and lots of raw goat meat. The Socotri used to raise civets for a secretion that was used in exotic perfumes; that's why they were introduced from India. But Weasel has had his musk glands removed. Otherwise you wouldn't be holding him on your lap right now." Julia laughed.

"So, were you kidding in your letter when you said he was a cave explorer?"

"On the contrary—Weasel is our secret weapon. He can shimmy into the tightest holes or swim through flooded chambers. He isn't afraid of the dark and has an uncanny ability to find his way back through any underground maze. We're hoping that you might be able to rig a little apparatus that Weasel could wear—like an old-fashioned miner's light, but with one of your tiny videocams."

"Sure, that should be no problem. But I hope he doesn't add my microbats to his diet."

"Oh, he tried to eat my camera once, but now he's strictly carnivorous."

14. THE BADW

The final segment of the drive was a torturous climb up a boulder-strewn streambed. The Land Rovers' engines whined in protest as their drivers shifted into the lowest gears of four-wheel drive. The pickup gamely followed behind them. Occasionally they scattered the dwarf cattle that were unique to the island or goats browsing on thornbrush.

At last they emerged onto a plateau surrounded on three sides by towering red granite peaks that seemed literally to erupt from the underlying limestone. On the hillsides were astonishing groves of dragon's blood (*Dracaena cinnabari*), resembling giant mushrooms or inside-out umbrellas, as well as grotesque "cucumber trees" and gnarled tamarinds.

The occasional frankincense tree, with its strong-smelling yellowish sap, hinted at ancient glory. Julia explained to Jack that the incense burned in the Temple of Solomon and at the Oracle in Delphi, as well as that borne by the Magi as gifts to Bethlehem—all came from these extraordinary hill forests of Socotra.

Looking back, Jack had a spectacular view of the Hadibo Plain and the gray-blue Indian Ocean. Here and there they could see tiny red dots on the water: fishermen in their *lateen*-sail *sambuqs*.

The convoy reached camp. "Camp Terbec," as it was called, consisted of Samira's clinic, with accommodations for mothers and children; Hasan's and Julia's lab; Anwar's tiny office filled with communications equipment; and a primitively furnished bunkroom where Jack and Conor would share quarters with Weasel. A nearby spring had been siphoned into a pool to provide bathing facilities.

Julia boarded with Hasan and Samira in their modest cottage. A small garden, fenced against goats, doubled as Omar's playground. Anwar, meanwhile, took one of the Land Rovers home every night to the main UN compound in Hadibo. The villagers, great believers in vampires, had warned him to keep his windows rolled up when he drove around the island at night.[8]

Tariq and Hadad, meanwhile, lived with their young families just across the stream in the extraordinary village of Terbec. While the coastal population, of mixed African and Hadrami ancestry, dwelt in gypsum-plastered cubes of brick and coral, the highland Socotri, or *badw*, the island's indigenous people, were still true "troglodytes": they were cave dwellers.

Tariq and Hadad, to be sure, had built a tin-covered garage for their truck, as well as a concrete house for the village's new oil-fueled electrical generator (donated by the Dutch government). But otherwise, the inhabitants of Terbec, along with their goats, sheep, cattle, and fleas, still slept soundly in their ancestral caves, the best shelter against the winds that cursed Socotra like nowhere else on earth.

Now the villagers gathered around the Land Rovers to sing a traditional greeting to their new guests from Ireland as musicians drummed and played tambourines. A festival had been organized.

Jack and Conor were enraptured by the reception. "Whoa, a *hooley!*" said Conor.

They got out of the vehicles and exchanged the traditional greeting by touching noses and clasping hands. Everyone was talking at once in Socotri.

Socotri, dauntingly difficult to speak, is an ancient, mysterious, unwritten language related to Mahari, a dialect spoken in eastern Yemen. A turn-of-the-century naturalist fluent in Arabic was entirely baffled by it. "In subtlety of sound Socotri is painfully rich. They corkscrew their tongues, gurgle in their throats and bring sounds from alarming depths . . ."[9]

Indeed, during the entire period—from 1886 to 1967—when Socotra was a British protectorate, no European ever managed to speak the language. Hasan, however, had become reasonably proficient, and Julia—fluent in Hebrew and Arabic—had acquired a smattering. Part of the problem was the lack of a Socotri dictionary, a necessity if the language were to survive the predicted onslaught of visitors.

The villagers had organized a traditional highland feast: tangy goat stew, kebabs of roasted lamb, huge platters of rice with *ghee*, pomegranates and fresh dates, and endless *rawbah* (sour milk fermented in a goatskin). Samira explained that unlike the coastal Socotri, who ate fish and garden vegetables, the highland *badw* were almost completely pastoral. Until recently, when subsidized imported rice had become popular, their diet was virtually starchless; dates took the place of bread, but goat, mutton, and above all, *rawbah*, remained dietary mainstays.

"This really is a bit of paradise, isn't it," Conor whispered to Jack.

"Yeah, but look how thin the people are."

Indeed, the *badw*—a handsome, biblical-looking people—did appear undernourished. Babies' ribs poked through their chests, and older women's faces were drawn tight around the skull. Everyone ate with amazing gusto.

Samira overheard the brothers' conversation.

"Until recently, infant mortality in the highlands was nearly 30 percent. You're visiting in a good season during a fat year. Often there are floods, followed by long droughts. The *badw* first watch their goats die, then their babies."

"Wouldn't it make sense to build more of an agricultural base?" asked Jack.

"Of course, but that requires a dependable water supply for irrigation. As you'll see in the next few weeks, the mountains catch immense amounts of rainfall, but there is little soil to retain it. Like other karst landscapes, the rain percolates straight into limestone and seems lost forever. I suppose it flows through caves and then back to the sea."

"That's why our cave exploration has a double mission." Dr. Hasan broke in. "While you three are looking for salamanders and crickets, I'll be water prospecting. The Belgian speleologists who were here last fall think that Socotra may have a wealth of underground lakes and streams."

"A mixed blessing." Anwar spoke in English.

"What do you mean?" asked Jack.

"Water has competing uses. The central government in San'a would love to see Socotra as—how do you say in America?—yes, as a 'cash cow.' Water would sustain new development: tourism and commercial agriculture. It's unclear what benefit would flow to the Socotri themselves. The Galapagos Islands are usually offered as a model for the future of Socotra, but in the Galapagos almost all the tourist income is captured by the big tour operators. The local fishermen make next to nothing."

"Anwar is right," Hasan said. "New water resources could simply accelerate the tourist development of the island. Arab- and English-speaking workers would be imported and the native Socotri either reduced to rustic curiosities, or worse, forced to emigrate."

"Yes, something similar has happened to many of the island communities of the west of Ireland." Conor was talking. "I suppose it's a worldwide trend: the tourists get the beautiful beaches and the locals get one-way tickets to the mainland."

"So why are we looking for water if it won't help the Socotri?" Jack once again found science caught on the horns of a moral dilemma.

"Because it could be an enormous blessing," Hassan replied. "It might preserve the Socotri way of life as well as help save their babies. But it all depends on the *badw* themselves. Our responsibility is to survey the island's biodiversity and natural resources. It's up to them to decide what to make out of the competing potentials."

"But what if they decide to cash out, to sell their traditional way of life for something a tad bit more comfortable and healthier for their kids? What if the *badw*, say, cut a deal with the big players, Club Med or Disney, and let them take over the island? Doesn't the United Nations—and don't we as scientists—still have a moral mandate to protect this unique biodiversity?" Jack was thinking out loud.

"I take your point, Jack," said Dr. Hasan. "But the Socotri have been fairly responsible guardians of this ecosystem for several thousand years. Their cultural survival and the survival of the biome go hand in hand. Each is equally endangered and equally sacred. Ask Tariq and Hadad what they think."

Dr. Hasan translated the gist of the conversation for the two men. Julia then translated their responses for Jack and Conor.

"They say they want three things. First, a more secure food supply to ensure their children's health. Second, decent bilingual schools teaching both Arabic and Socotri. And third, their extraordinary island home—its reefs, mountains, caves, and mangrove swamps—left intact as testament to the glory of Allah."

"But how do they propose to ensure those goals? What real clout, if any, do they have over multinational corporations, the central government in San'a, or even the local officials down in Hadibo?" Jack was still playing the devil's advocate.

Tariq and Hadad talked and then translated the questions into Socotri for benefit of the other villagers; a heated discussion ensued. Finally Tariq reported the consensus.

"Yes, this is a problem. We're not a warrior people, not like the Yemeni or Somali tribes. For thousands of years we have settled our disputes non-violently—we don't make war on strangers. Indeed, our ancestors took to these caves to flee first the Greeks, then the Portuguese, followed by the Wahabis—Saudis—and finally the British. But they didn't stay. We've defeated our invaders by simply outlasting them."

Hadad now interrupted. "Of course, we understand the present situation is radically different. Suddenly our poor land has great value. We knew something fundamental had changed when the new airport was built. And when we first started seeing the American soldiers in the mountains."

Jack and Julia exchanged nervous looks.

It was Tariq's turn again. "So we hope that by embracing the 'friendly people of all tribes' (he meant the United Nations), others will know the justice of what we seek. We're very happy to have had so many wise men and women come to our mountains in recent years."

"But what do you mean about American soldiers?" Conor had an image of their friend in sunglasses.

Dr. Hasan answered. "I'm afraid that question will answer itself over the next few weeks as we travel around the island. But for the present, let's drink *rawbah* and make merry. Tomorrow we're up at six and headed for Hoq Cave."

Hasan lifted his curdled milk in a toast to the kind but anxious villagers of Terbec.

15. KISS THE CIVET

Goat fleas tormented Jack and Conor all night long, but they took consolation in the fact that they were in the cool highlands, away from the biting sand flies and swamp mosquitoes that gave Hadibo such a dreadful reputation.

After a quick breakfast of *rawbah*, weak tea, cornflakes, and a couple slices of Julia's glorious date bread, the expedition was ready to test Jack's microbats in actual cave conditions. The team had to drive back down the mountain to the Habido Plain, then pick up a rough road that led to the villages on the northeast coast.

They bumped along for an hour or so until they reached the trailhead. Tariq and Hadad volunteered to help carry the microwave gear, but it was still a cumbersome burden on the steep mountain trail.

"Jack, couldn't you have miniaturized some of this gear? This is like lugging a color television up Mt. Everest." Conor was in a sweat.

"Come on now, Junior, you're in better condition than I am." Jack was being honest. The year and a half of late-night work in the Caltech labs had left him out of shape and out of breath.

Julia laughed. She not only shouldered her share of the load, but she also carried Weasel in one of Omar's old baby pouches.

"Weasel, don't you feel sorry for these poor Irish weaklings?"

"Julia, I swear, that damn civet is grinning." Jack was still amazed by Weasel's responses to conversation.

"Evil, lazy, rat-sucking mongoose." Conor swore under his breath.

"Conor! Not another word out of you or Weasel will jump out of his pouch and bite your nose off. Never, never call a civet a mongoose," Julia mock-scolded.

"Apologize," urged Jack.

"OK, I apologize." Conor cautiously petted the civet's head. "Weasel, me lad, you're the pride of the tribe, the handsomest of civet cats. But you're still as useless as a chocolate teapot, you lazy beggar."

Julia kicked Conor. "You're so ornery. First you say bad things about baseball, then you insult my civet."

"Conor flunked charm school," added Jack.

Dr. Hasan overheard the exchange. "Don't worry," he smiled, "neither of you are getting off this island alive until you learn to kiss a civet and can recite the batting order of the Mets."

16. "MORPHY" MAKES GOOD

Hoq took their breath away. The cave was located just under the crest of a limestone plateau three miles from the sea. The opening was huge: two hundred yards wide and one hundred yards high.

"That's one fierce big cave," Jack muttered to Conor.

"Aye, big enough to fly a jumbo jet through." Conor mounted a telescopic lens on his digital camera.

"Can we have a gander first?" Jack asked Dr. Hasan.

"No, it would spoil the experiment. I don't want you to have any idea of what's inside the cave. Let's set up your equipment and see whether your bat can find its way. Then we'll go inside and have lunch."

As everyone crowded around, Jack carefully explained the function and assembly of the portable microwave transmitter. Julia translated for Hadad and Tariq.

The apparatus consisted of a two-foot-diameter parabolic antenna and three transmitter units (TXUs) stacked on top of each other on a sturdy tripod, with a coaxial cable connection to Jack's laptop and a power hookup to the batteries in one of the backpacks.

"This is virtually the same equipment that television crews use to receive and transmit video images from the field." Jack pushed a function key on his laptop and the stacked TXUs began to purr. "The difference is that we use the microwaves to feed power to our hungry little microbats. But with a second antenna, we could also transmit images from the tiny videocams in the bats' noses."

"So you need one of these setups to power each bat?" Tariq asked.

"No, it's much better than that. This system is capable of launching an entire 'swarm.'

"As many as a dozen MAVs—little drones like the bats—can be flown on one broad beam. Moreover, by simultaneously broadcasting at different frequencies—low band and high band together—we can power the swarm as a whole while guiding the individual movements of each bat. We successfully tested this in Pasadena ten days ago."

The technical details of microbat choreography were over the heads of the three bioscience types, as well as Hadad. But Tariq—the only civilian on Socotra who understood the electronics in a Land Rover engine—nodded enthusiastically. Jack had at least one eager convert.

"OK, Jack, this sounds brilliant. But where are your furry little long-eared friends from California?" Dr. Hasan was just as eager as everyone else to see the famous MAVs.

Jack carefully opened a stainless steel box, gently extracted "Morphy," the prize performer from the Mt. Wilson trials, and passed the little microbat around.

His tiny body was fabricated from carbon fiber and clear plastic with embedded gum-stick-like lithium-polymer batteries and strands of copper antennae. The wings were made out of a novel "shape metal" piezoelectric alloy that alternately stiffened and flexed in obedience to signals from the ground. The flapping motion for hovering and slow flight was generated by tiny twin motors at the base of each wing; the motors, in turn, operated dual carbon-fiber cam arms. Morphy was exquisitely designed, the robotic equivalent of a fine Swiss watch.

"Wow, Jack, I remember when you used to doodle designs like this a few years ago. He's a knockout." Conor beamed in admiration.

"Almost as cute as a civet," said Julia, as Weasel snarled jealously at the strange creature.

"Shall we begin?" Jack pulled a second laptop out of another pack and hooked it up. "OK, Conor, lay Morphy on that bit of open ground near that pomegranate tree. Thanks."

Jack, who sat on a rock facing the cave, typed furiously into his laptop while the others gathered around the second laptop and waited for something to happen. In response to one of Jack's commands, the parabolic antenna moved and the second screen came to life.

Then the tiny prop on Morphy's rear end started whirling at an impossible speed and his wings flexed. Suddenly, he took off.

"My god, it actually flies," exclaimed Dr. Hasan.

"Look at the screen," said Hadad in Arabic. It was a bat's-eye view of the terrain.

Jack flew Morphy straight at the overhanging cliff face at an increasing speed.

"Watch it, Jack, you're gonna splatter him!" Conor was horrified.

At the last second, Morphy shot straight up, folded his wings close to his body, and somersaulted into a perfect 360-degree roll: he then banked sharply, spread his wings open, and headed toward the ocean. It gave Julia motion sickness to watch the acrobatics on the screen.

Jack now turned Morphy around and again sent him hurtling toward the cave. He abruptly stopped in front of the opening and hovered triumphantly.

"Bravo, Jack, quite a show," said Hasan. The others just applauded.

"OK, now comes the hard part. Dr. Hasan, please put these on and tell me where you want Murphy to go."

Jack handed the team leader a pair of virtual reality (VR) video glasses that gave Dr. Hasan the same view as the robotic bat's videocam.

Jack hit a key and a tiny but powerful laser shone from Morphy's nose. Jack used the mouse on his laptop to aim the synchronized light beam and videocam. Like an old-fashioned flashlight lens, he could modulate the beam to weakly illuminate very broad swaths or more intensely light up smaller areas.

"This is incredible," gushed Dr. Hasan. "It's exactly like being in the cave myself." The others had to settle for the two-dimensional picture on the laptop screen.

"I have to be careful," explained Jack. "I don't want him smashing against anything. I've brought audio sensors—almost replicating those used by a real bat—that will automatically alert Morphy to imminent collision, but I haven't attached them yet. I will also probably need to reduce his wingspan so he can fit into tighter places."

"I wouldn't worry about that now. He has loads of room." Conor was slack-jawed at the images on the screen.

Morphy's videocam showed why Hoq Cave—first systematically explored by the Belgians in 2001—had already acquired a cult reputation amongst spelunkers and adventure tourists. Like the interior of some wondrous gothic cathedral, the cave's vast chambers contained immense speleotherm sculptures, including soaring stalagmites that resembled the minarets of San'a, stalactites that hung from the ceiling like giant swords, and intricate wall tapestries of gypsum flowers.

The team—except for Hadad, who was frightened by the seemingly magical equipment—took turns looking through the sensational VR glasses as little Morphy penetrated deeper into the one-mile-long system.

Deep inside the cave, Morphy sent back images of ancient footprints calcified in the cave floor. He was in the room where archaeologists from Collège de France had recently discovered early Christian artifacts, including pottery, incense holders, and two wooden tablets covered with engraved inscriptions in Aramaic, the language of Christ.

Never before had a ceremonial space been discovered so deep inside a cave. The archaeologists speculated that Hoq had probably been an international shrine of Christian mysticism, and indeed, wall inscriptions in different languages attested to visitors from as far away as India, Egypt, and Cyprus; most dated from the third century, when the ancestors of today's *badw* had been Nestorian Christians.

Finally, after two hours of bravura adventure, Jack recalled his little bat. The entire video stream recorded by Morphy was stored in Jack's computer and transformed into map data. To bring Morphy back, Jack simply had to press another function key.

Ten minutes later, the MAV was fluttering above their heads. Jack programmed Morphy to hover close to Weasel, who again bared his teeth and hissed at this intruder who had become the new center of attention. The team again applauded.

"Well done, Jack. Now our only problem is to convince Weasel to become friends with Morphy." Dr. Hasan laughed.

17. HASAN'S PLAN

The team put on laser headlights and entered the cavern. They ate lunch in the immense auditorium of the main gallery, taking extreme care not to damage any of the delicate speleothems. Their conversation echoed between stalagmites and then faded away in the interior chambers.

Julia and Conor, on their hands and knees, mucked around the edge of a dark pool.

"What are you looking for?" Hadad asked in Arabic.

"Oh, the Belgians discovered a new species of *Isopoda* a few years ago. We're just searching for some," Julia replied.

"To eat?" Hadad was vaguely horrified.

"No, to put in bottles, you silly shepherd. They're scientists." Tariq playfully punched his cousin on the arm and Hadad chuckled.

Dr. Hasan let everyone relax for a few more minutes, then he called the team meeting to order.

"I want to explain our fieldwork schedule for the next two weeks." He paused so that Julia could translate into Arabic.

"We need a few more days back at Terbec to sort out logistics and equipment. Jack wants to outfit his bats with audiosensors, and Julia needs help devising a videocam rig for Weasel. Tariq will go to town with Anwar to procure a boat for the trip around the coast.

"Meanwhile, I would like Conor to organize a climbing clinic for the rest of us. In addition to his role as the team paleontologist, I'm appointing him chief guide. All decisions having to do with technical climbing, route-finding, and team safety will be deferred to him. OK?"

"Absolutely," said Jack and Julia in unison. Both remembered Conor's fearless expertise in the treacherous conditions of Greenland.

"I want Tariq and Hadad to practice climbing with Conor as well. Although they won't be going on our expedition to the unexplored karst region of southwestern Socotra, it is essential that they have some technical climbing skills—in a real emergency, we might have to call upon them to rescue us."

Tariq and Hadad nodded eagerly. The climbing sounded like fun. Both wished they could accompany the expedition, but they had babies and broken motors at home. They would, however, monitor the team's progress by radio from Terbec.

"So, Dr. Hasan, we'll be heading out by boat this weekend for the southwest?" Julia was beaming with excitement.

"No. I am going to postpone our departure by another week."

"But why?" Julia was crestfallen.

Dr. Hasan laughed. "Julia, don't look so unhappy. I have another adventure planned for you first. You'll be delighted."

"What's that?"

"We're going to Ras Momi to talk to a witch about dragons."

CHAPTER FOUR: *Ras Momi*

And you must know that on this island there are the best enchanters in the world.
MARCO POLO, *writing about Socotra*[10]

Witchcraft is not accepted or recognised in any form in Islam but it is not surprising to find it on Socotra—it is not really surprising to find anything on Socotra.
OXFORD UNIVERSITY EXPEDITION (1956)[11]

18. A BRIGHT IDEA

Conor's climbing class was a greater success than anyone had anticipated. He had scheduled "elementary rappel and belay technique" for 9 A.M. in front of a nearby limestone butte. When Tariq and Hadad showed up, a bit late, they were accompanied by a huge gaggle of children and teenagers.

Conor was atop the butte with Julia and Jack; it took him less than a minute to rappel down the two-hundred-foot-high cliff.

"Good. Good." The children clapped as they practiced one of the English words that Samira had taught them. "Very, very good."

Conor smiled.

"Please," asked Tariq in halting English. "Climb again. The kids want to see."

Conor was happy to oblige. Using the strong, smooth technique he had honed on the boulders and sea cliffs of Ireland, he rapidly made his way up a large crack. When that gave out, he neatly traversed to another, smaller crack and inserted a chock for protection. Suddenly he heard Jack shouting from the top.

He looked up, but Jack was pointing downward with alarm. "The kids, the kids," Jack was screaming.

Conor looked below and was horrified to see that all the village children were nonchalantly ascending the big crack—evidently they thought this was a game of follow-the-leader. He felt faint.

Then he noticed that the kids' style was flawless. They were using fist-jams and laybacks as if they were second nature. Moreover, they were climbing barefoot, while he was wearing an expensive pair of La Sportiva rock shoes. Like other mountain people, the *badw* probably learned to climb before they learned to walk.

However, he had to stop them before they reached the dangerous traverse. He established a fail-safe belay point, then doubled his rope through it. He rappelled down to the highest child, a curly-haired girl of about ten, who gave him a dimpled smile.

Pretending this was all a wonderful game, he wound the rope

around her waist, and then, with one strong arm holding her and the other arm grasping the rope, he quickly rappelled to the base of the cliff. The other kids cheered and started clamoring something in Socotri, which Conor assumed meant: "My turn! My turn!"

By this time Jack and Julia understood Conor's plan, and both rappelled down on their separate lines to rescue other children. Within ten minutes everyone was safely back on the ground.

Julia explained to Tariq and Hadad what had happened; they had seemingly not recognized the peril. Deeply embarrassed, they began to apologize.

Conor, who was very agitated, told Julia that they all needed to return to camp immediately and hold a meeting.

A few minutes later, everyone was gathered around the picnic table in front of the clinic. Dr. Hasan and Samira had joined them, along with Anwar. Tariq and Hadad hung their heads in shame, worried that their jobs—and even worse, their reputations—were at stake.

Julia recounted in Arabic what had happened at the cliff face, how some of the children had climbed a full eighty feet before anyone could react. She emphasized that several children could have been killed or seriously injured. As she spoke, Hadad had tears on his cheeks.

"This is indeed a serious incident," Dr. Hasan began. "Conor, thanks for being so quick-witted and skillful. You prevented disaster this morning. As our safety expert, what lesson should we learn from this?" Samira repeated this in Arabic.

Conor stood up. His eyes were blazing. "Don't you realize what happened today?"

Hadad slunk into his seat, a broken man. Tariq, equally abject, slumped in his chair.

The question hung in the air. Then Conor supplied his own answer. "We've discovered the secret of how Terbec can improve the health of its children, generate new income, and at the same time, conserve the environment." Conor threw his hands over his head like a fiery young prophet.

Dr. Hasan's jaw dropped, and Hadad and Tariq recovered their posture.

"What on earth are you talking about?" Jack was afraid that Conor had suffered a brain hernia in the rescue.

"Look, did you see those kids climb? I mean, they were absolutely fearless, with perfect balance and a wonderful feel for the rock. I'm sure they could have climbed to the top without a second thought. And that was a hard 5.9 route that few of my friends in the UCD rock-climbing club would have ever attempted without a rope."

"Yeah, Conor, the kids here are little mountain goats, but so what?" Samira didn't know what to make of the younger brother.

"But don't you see? With some proper equipment and climbing classes, some of the local kids could become first-class professional guides."

Conor's jigsaw puzzle suddenly arranged itself into a clear pattern for Jack.

"So your idea is that Terbec could become a base camp for trekkers, with professional local guides who would ensure that the local culture was respected and that minimal damage was done to any of the native ecosystems."

"Exactly. You have some of the best raw climbing talent in the world here."

Dr. Hasan furrowed his brow, then unfurrowed it. "Actually, this may just be a brilliant idea. Hadad, Tariq, what do you think?"

Julia explained to them that in the faraway cold countries—Nunavut and Greenland—where Conor had spent so much time, local people had built new livelihoods by operating hostels and providing guide services. It gave them more control over the impact of tourism and modernization.

"How would you organize something like this?" Hadad asked.

"As a cooperative." Tariq now took the initiative. "The same way we have always organized the rotation of our goats and sheep in the pastures or have planned village celebrations. All together. Everyone contributing something and everyone sharing the benefits. But some of our youngsters would need to learn the climbing techniques and the science talk. They would also need to speak Arabic, and probably English. How would this be done? Who would help us?"

Everyone looked at Dr. Hasan, then at Conor. But it was Anwar, the quiet bookkeeper, who answered first.

"We could apply for grants from the environmental agencies. Samira is already teaching some English to the kids. Maybe we could find a young schoolteacher in Hadibo who would be willing to come live with us. If he or she doesn't speak it, you could teach him or her Socotri while your children are taught in Arabic." No one had ever seen Anwar so enthused.

"And how about science, biology, mountaineering, cave exploring . . .," wondered Hadad.

Anwar had an answer. "Well, while they're here for the next six months, Dr. Hasan and Samira can teach the kids about their environment. Tariq is already showing some of them how machines work. And perhaps this young Irishman could provide a few weeks of climbing instruction."

"More than that," Conor's eyes were sparkling. "I'm sure I could get the UCD rock-climbing club to partner with Terbec. We could send you ropes, shoes, helmets, and climbing gear."

"Caltech could help set up a website," Jack volunteered.

"And Columbia could provide other technical assistance, maybe even organize a regular field school," Julia added.

"Anwar and I will start writing a proposal for the UN. OK?" Dr. Hasan looked at Tariq and Hadad. They smiled their assent.

Later, Tariq would compare Conor to one of the traditional waterfinders who went from village to village, helping people locate springs and underground waters. Out of the unexpected aquifer of friendship, a new dream had bubbled up from the ancient limestone of Terbec.

19. A PREVALENCE OF WITCHES

The night before the planned expedition to Ras Momi, Dr. Hasan tripped in the dark and sprained his ankle. An emergency team meeting was called.

Dr. Hasan was lying on a couch with an icepack on his injured ankle and Omar on his chest. "What a revolting development this is," he complained.

"Should we postpone the trip?" Julia asked.

"Not on your life. Here, Jack, help me up. Conor, please take Omar."

Dr. Hasan staggered to his desk. A large satellite photo of Socotra was spread across it.

"Forgive me if I seem to lecture, but I need to give you the full background."

He used a pencil to point to land features on the photo.

"As you know, Socotra consists of three principal landscapes. There are coastal plains here, around Hadibo and in the south; here, the granite Haghir Mountains that tower above Terbec; and the majority of the island, which is uplifted limestone one thousand to two thousand feet above sea level. This upland is dissected by deep streams that divide it into three segments: the eastern, central, and western plateaus."

Weasel yawned and curled up in a corner.

"Now, the legends—or if you prefer, the stories—about dragons are all from the west of the island. Indeed, the people around here, or further east, take no heed of these stories at all. They believe in vampires, genies, and witches, but not in dragons."

"So why are we going to Ras Momi at the far eastern end of Socotra, if the dragon caves are in the west?" Conor was confused.

"Come closer." Hasan had everyone peering at the southwestern corner of the island. "Do you see these great sea cliffs? Some are almost nine hundred feet high. There are huge, inaccessible, and unexplored cave openings all along this cliff face for about five miles, but only one formerly inhabited spot—right here."

"Formerly inhabited?" Julia asked.

"Yes, a tiny cliff dwelling, a village called Amia. The people there were known as dragon hunters, pirates, and sorcerers, and they were greatly feared by other Socotri."

"What happened to them?"

"Six years ago the Yemeni military forcibly removed the population to the southern plain."

"Why?" puzzled Conor.

"Because Amia was the birthplace, and indeed the military believed the base, of the most notorious pirate in the Gulf of Aden."

"Kaitos?" said Jack and Conor in unison.

Dr. Hasan chuckled. "I see his reputation has spread far and wide. Yes, the giant pirate Kaitos, who is rumored to be grotesquely deformed, with hands and feet but no arms or legs. He's supposedly carried around in a divan chair by his fanatic followers, who more or less worship him as a wizard. The Yemeni navy is still combing the coastline looking for his new hideout."

"But what does this have to do with Ras Momi?" Julia was persistent.

"Well, Kaitos has a sister. The other villagers denounced her as a witch. A *zahra*. Do you know anything about witchcraft on Socotra?"

"A little." Conor had read the scant English-language literature on the island. "Socotra was famous since Greek times for its magicians and sorcerers. Marco Polo claimed they could change the weather or make themselves invisible. I've also read that witches were once thrown off the same sea cliffs that you are pointing to.

"Good, Conor. Anyone else?"

Julia had read the same three books as Conor. "I think that practice was reformed in the eighteenth or nineteenth century. Instead of executing witches, the Socotrans tried them by ordeal and exiled them to the mainland of south Arabia."

Hasan continued. "Indeed, 'witches' were still being put on public trial as late as 1955. They were weighted with rocks and thrown into the sea. If they sank, they were pulled up and thrown in again. If they managed to float or struggle to the surface, they were judged guilty and banished.[12] Banishment to the mainland was prohibited in the 1970s by the revolutionary regime in Aden, but they could not stop the local people from ostracizing supposed witches. Thus, Kaitos's sister was driven from village to village, until she at last found refuge in the loneliest place in Socotra—here, on the notorious peninsula of Ras Momi, where she has only hungry crabs and the ghosts of dead sailors for company."

"Isn't this where the *Ryukyu Rainbow* ran aground and exploded in a giant fireball?" Jack asked rather nervously.

"Yes. And you'll leave for there tomorrow, by the most direct route, over the eastern plateau. It's a long two-day hike, but Tariq will accompany you halfway. And we'll be in constant radio contact."

"And our mission?" asked Conor.

"Interview Kaitos's sister. I am told she speaks Arabic, so Julia will have no problem conversing with her. She knows all about the so-called 'dragons' and can provide us with invaluable information about the cliff caves."

"But why should she talk to us? And what do we do if she simply tells us to buzz off?" asked Jack.

"Well, we obviously can't coerce this poor, persecuted woman to talk. But I am sending along a backpack full of gifts—candles, rice, fishing line, and so on. Hopefully this will allay her fears and win her friendship. Any other questions?"

"What's the route like?" asked Conor, the chief guide.

"The usual for Socotra: a horrible, poorly marked trail over the mountains and across the plain. You'll run into torrential rain and gale-force winds. Pretty much 'normal' weather."

"Sounds like home," chuckled Conor.

"Oh, one more thing." Hasan returned to the couch. "Take advantage of this pleasant hike to look for potholes, cracks, or other evidence of caves. The Belgians have pretty much surveyed this part of the island, but you never know."

"Yeah, I read on their website that they estimate that barely 1 percent of the island's caves have actually been discovered or explored." Jack was excited by the prospect of stumbling on something like the cavern at Hoq. "Should I bring the bat equipment?"

"No, too much weight. But do take along Weasel with his new videocam headwear. You'll be pleasantly surprised by his spelunking abilities." Hasan smiled at Julia, then his face darkened a bit.

"Be careful. The Socotri, on every occasion, will be hospitable and generous, but there is a chance you may run into one of the 'anti-terrorist' patrols—Yemeni army, Americans, or both. Be very polite and cautious about your language. And keep in regular radio contact with camp. *Ma'a s-salama.*"

20. NEW FRIENDS

The group left at dawn the next morning. It was chilly, and the Haghir spires were hidden by low clouds.

"This landscape looks like our own Mountains of Mourne on LSD," quipped Jack.

Conor laughed.

The country beyond Terbec did resemble a strangely morphed or distorted version of Irish mountain country. The trees and succulents were unnaturally obese, almost as if they had been pumped full of fluid to the verge of exploding. The *Adenium* and *Dendrosicyos* (cucumber trees), especially, looked like the rotten bloated flesh of drowned men or dead sea creatures. Conor shuddered at the similarity.

This was the first time that the kids had been alone with Tariq, and they relished Julia's translations of his stories and jokes. Like all Socotri, he had an incredible knowledge of the island's unique and sometimes bizarre flora. There were almost three hundred endemic plants growing nowhere else in the world, and Tariq seemed to know of a medicinal function or practical use for each of them.

Pointing at the low forest of dragon's blood and wild orange trees surrounding them, he said, "You may think this just wilderness, but to us Socotri it is really—how do you say?—a 'supermarket.' All these plants are friends."

Tariq had taken the eerie edge off the morning and made the kids feel comfortable in this strange, primordial forest.

At the first rest stop, Jack sat on a rock while he emptied gravel from his hiking boots.

"For godsakes, Jack, watch out!" Conor yelled.

Jack jumped up and looked at his feet. An absolutely enormous centipede, about ten inches long, crawled over his sock and disappeared under another rock.

"What in the heck was that?"

This time Julia didn't laugh. "A centipede, but a little bit bigger than most. Ugh!"

Conor was surprised. He had never seen Julia recoil from any creature. She hugged polar bears, took spiders to bed, and domesticated civets. She was the most fearless person he knew.

"Julia, are you actually afraid of centipedes?"

"Well, I got stung by one last month. It's often compared to a gunshot wound, but actually I think it was worse. There's no treatment—you just put ice on the wound and hope you die quickly. Really, the first few hours were sheer agony."

Jack gulped at his close call. "Are there many centipedes on Socotra?"

Julia translated for Tariq. He laughed uproariously and then began to systematically turn over every nearby rock. Without exception, a fiercely beautiful giant centipede—fiery red or more startling, bright blue—emerged.

Conor wished he could stand on a stool or be evacuated by helicopter, while Jack just wanted to wake up: this was obviously a nightmare.

"Well, guys," said Julia, "you now see the scale of the problem. Forget the fleas, mosquitoes, and sand flies: the centipedes are the real glory of Socotra. Every visitor since the ancient Greeks has been horrified by their prevalence.[13] The only thing possibly worse are the attack crabs."

"Attack crabs?" Jack asked incredulously.

Julia translated for Tariq, who again doubled up in laughter.

"Don't worry, you won't have to deal with the crabs until tomorrow." Tariq smiled serenely.

Just to make sure it wasn't all a hallucination, Conor randomly kicked over another rock. It was an even bigger blue monster than the one that almost stung Jack.

"Can we sleep in the trees tonight?"

21. SUPERSTITIONS

They camped in the mouth of a large but shallow cave that obviously had been used by people for centuries; its roof was black with smoke, and Conor found potsherds that Julia identified as medieval. Fortunately, the cave seemed to be unpopular with centipedes, although there were huge spiders spinning yellow webs and the usual occupying army of goat fleas.

By campfire, they talked more about Conor's ideas about mountain guides and locally controlled tourism.

Tariq was enthusiastic, although he was unsure whether it would be approved by the central government. Only in recent years had the presence of San'a actually been felt in the mountains. The badw were suspicious of policies made outside their own local, broadly participative councils, and Tariq expressed the opinion that they should be left alone to govern themselves.

But he was no zealot of violent independence. He had witnessed terrible scenes in Yemen during the civil war in the early 1990s: on his way to Saudi Arabia, he had seen the bodies of civilians stacked like cordwood in Aden City, and the memory haunted him. He hated war, even for a noble cause.

"Do you have wars on your island?" he asked his Irish friends.

"For five hundred years only," answered Jack. "We were the first colony of England. Cowboys and Indians was invented in Ireland—and we were the original Indians."

Julia told Tariq briefly about the massacres, deportations, executions, and famines that embittered the Irish.

Tariq shook his head. "Do you have pirates as well?"

"These days we call them 'entrepreneurs,'" Conor offered. Julia translated the idea.

Tariq laughed. "Yes, I understand. We call them 'land pirates': rich men who cheat the poor; dishonest merchants; and sheiks who scorn the Koran with their sloth and greed. But seriously, do you have real pirates as well?"

"Once upon a time we did—great pirates, especially in the West of our island. Most often they were poor fishermen who took to piracy when the English government tried to drive them off the sea. Some were women."

"Yes, the same here. Most pirates are actually Somali or Yemeni fishermen. Some Socotri as well, but not *badw*; we are not a sea people. We do not like guns. Trucks and cars I like very much. But not guns."

"How about Kaitos?" asked Conor.

"He's a monster, truly. Most pirates leave local people alone, but Kaitos is incredibly angry. He kidnaps *badw*, and when we cannot pay ransom, we never see friends again. Yet other times he comes with gifts. No one understands Kaitos. No one can predict his behavior."

Conor was puzzled. "Why hasn't the government been able to catch him, if he is such a notorious menace?"

"Because he has powerful magic. He comes from a race of sorcerers, and his sister is a *zahra*, a witch. Be very careful when you meet her. She is greatly to be feared. I disagree with Dr. Hasan—I do not think it is a good idea for you to go Ras Momi."

"But Tariq, do you really believe in sorcery, witches, and all that? I mean, you are the most modern man amongst the *badw*. You understand engines, electronics, even microwaves. You can read and write. Shouldn't you set an example and help dispel these superstitions?" Jack was fervent.

Tariq narrowed his eyes as Julia translated. "Jack, maybe on your island people are not 'superstitious,' as you call it. Maybe you no longer have pirates or witches, maybe you are completely modern, but we're not. And on Socotra there are two worlds: one above ground and one under it. Isn't that why you are here—to explore our underground world? I must warn you: it is a world governed by sorcery."

"And dragons?" Julia asked.

"Oh, I don't know about dragons. Those people on west side of Socotra, very ignorant *badw*. Very superstitious." Tariq winked.

The kids laughed and crawled into their sleeping bags. Weasel, as always, slept curled at Julia's feet. Occasionally one of his wicked eyes would briefly open or his foxlike nose would twitch: all his sensors were armed. On an island entirely without canines, he was the most faithful watchdog.

22. MORNING SONG

The next morning was gloomy and cold. Tariq left early so he could rejoin his family by noon; the kids were sorry to see their good friend and mentor go.

Julia checked in with Dr. Hasan by radio while Jack and Conor confirmed their location by GPS. The only topographical maps of Socotra were top-secret military property, so they tried to plot the day's route on an enlarged copy of the satellite photo. They selected a line of march that, hopefully, would not plunge off a cliff or end in a mangrove swamp.

The now-bare plateau was shrouded in a dismal fog. The relentless winds had stripped away the thin layer of soil, and the occasional ghostly dragon's blood trees grew right out of the limestone itself. Otherwise, there was only lichen. Even goats avoided this part of the island.

"Well, at least the wind is quiet today," said Julia reassuringly, as they tried to grope their way through the fog. "That's unusual."

"And creepy," added Conor, who did not like the sticky silence. "This is like hiking in a cemetery. Hey Jack, give us a wee song to bolster our courage."

Julia loved it when Jack struck up a tune. He had a beautiful voice, and his singing was as strong, clean, and effortless as Conor's rock climbing. It did tickle her, however, that Jack the pacifist always seemed to prefer martial songs about brave ministral boys or "bold Fenian men" gone off to battle against impossible odds.

This morning, however, Jack tried a love ballad: "I wish I had you in Carrickfergus," he sang. His tenor voice lifted the gloom.

But lest the mood become too romantic, Conor responded with an insane version of an ancient punk song by the Pogues. Weasel—a punk pet if there ever was one—snarled and hissed in unison.

The expedition stumbled onward.

23. THE BANSHEE MAN

Gradually grass and shrubs reappeared, and they saw their first goat, then another. The adventurers were approaching the edge of the plateau and several tiny coastal villages; people were probably close by.

Or banshees.

The howling started faintly, then grew louder and came nearer. It was somewhere between a death shriek and the devil's laughter. None of them had ever heard anything stranger or more uncanny.

Jack put his hand on Julia's shoulder. "What in the name of O'Reilly is that? The Hound of the Baskervilles?" Conor soon joined the protective huddle.

"Let's just stay calm," Julia said nervously.

"Maybe we should scream too," Conor suggested.

Suddenly a figure emerged from the fog: a wild, bearded man with disheveled hair who wore only a dirty loincloth. He staggered past the group, howling, and then disappeared again into the mist. His voice trailed off in the distance.

The kids were frozen in shock and disbelief.

"Did I really see that, or was I dreaming?" asked Conor.

"I think we're all dreaming," said Julia. "Let's get out of this mad fog as quick as we can."

They began to descend from the plateau, climbing down from one short shelf to another, treacherous going in the fog. The rocks here seemed sharper and cut into their soles.

After about ten minutes, they could hear the thundering of the sea, then light dramatically broke through the mist from below.

"Stop!" Conor grabbed Jack from behind and pulled him back from a precipice. Some rocks crumbled into the void. Jack shivered.

"That gave me a canary. Thanks, Conor."

They stood at the edge of a sheer cliff overlooking a beach where the Indian Ocean pounded the dunes with the heavy artillery of its winter swells. To their right, about a mile further on, was the dark promontory of Ras Momi, their destination.

"Nice spot for a picnic." Julia pulled some rations out of her bag.

Jack checked their position again on the GPS while Conor walked off to search for a feasible way down to the beach.

He returned ten minutes later. "There's a big gully. Lots of scree, but easy enough."

Julia handed him some of her date bread, to which both brothers were now addicted, and Jack passed him a fruit drink.

With their heavy backpacks, both Julia and Jack found the descent tricky, if not dangerous; only the odd shrub provided a handhold to brake an uncontrolled slide.

They winced as Conor glissaded by them at the speed of light. Like Silver Surfer, he expertly rode the avalanche of rock and debris to the bottom, then turned and bowed.

"Show-off!" Julia yelled, as she clung desperately to a sad-looking tree root.

24. THE ATTACK

Finally they were on the beach, but they were not alone. Two giant Egyptian vultures—what the locals called "al Baladiya Socotri," or "the cleanup men of Socotra"—were violently pulling apart the flesh of a dead seal. They paid no more attention to the three kids than had the madman in the fog.

"Nature, red in tooth and claw . . . ," Jack muttered.

Julia shrugged her shoulders. "Recycling," she corrected.

After another half-mile the sand dunes gradually yielded to hard cobble. The wind picked up, and salt spray stung their eyes. And they began to see a few crabs, then more.

Finally they were scrambling over larger boulders, slippery with algae, and wading through tidepools. Green crabs were everywhere now.

"Let's get away from this," said Conor, as he led them up another gully. It was a long climb.

They were now on the sandy peninsula of Ras Momi, the "Haunt of Sirens." Towering behind them was the massif of al-Jumjumah ("the Skull") and its sheer thousand-foot cliff. The witch's home was somewhere ahead, perhaps a quarter of a mile.

Most of the peninsula was barren sand. Instead of being covered with grass or shrubs, it was crawling with green crabs. "What are crabs doing up here?" Conor wondered.

The crabs were, on average, three or four inches in length, but there were also the occasional monsters, up to eight inches, sporting huge asymmetrical claws. They looked famished.

"I've never seen so many crabs in my life," gasped Jack, who had grown up on Dublin Bay. "These must be land crabs. I wonder what they eat?"

"Just think," said Conor licking his lips, "if we only had enough garlic and butter, yummy Crab Newburg for eternity."

"Why don't I feel hungry?" asked Julia, as she kicked off a large crab that had sunk its claw deep into the sole of her boot. "I think these are a species of *Xanthoidea*—they're carnivorous. They like to eat carrion and are notoriously bad-tempered."

"Yeah, Conor, maybe we're the food item on the menu here. Better mind your house." Jack hastened the pace. The crabs seemed to follow.

As Conor stopped to zip up his parka, Julia ran up behind him and pulled off three or four crabs that had immediately crept up his pants leg.

"Let's not stop. Come on, keep going," she urged.

The meat-eating crabs also increased their pace. They made a menacing clicking sound with their pincers; some of the bolder ones seemed almost to be snapping at their heels. Others managed to hitch a ride— Jack pulled a large specimen off Julia's arm and another off the top of her pack just as it was about to grasp her hair.

"Ouch!" Something clawed Jack's arm. As Julia turned to see what was wrong, she tripped over a rock and sprawled on her back. Weasel spilled out of his baby pouch.

It was a signal for a feeding frenzy amongst the crabs. By the hundreds, they converged on Julia and Weasel from all directions. The brave civet tried to defend Julia, but he was immediately overwhelmed by crazed crabs. A second later and Julia herself was submerged beneath a seething mass of green claws.

The two brothers pulled Julia to her feet and frantically pulled crabs off her. Her face was streaming with blood, and she seemed to be in shock.

But while Jack and Conor were tending to their friend, the crabs began to overrun them as well. Within a few minutes, all three were writhing under the relentless attack. Hungry crabs were in Jack's hair, on the back of Conor's neck, and trying to crawl into the front of Julia's shirt.

The kids were bleeding from dozens of tiny wounds, and the smell of blood only stoked the crabs' frenzy. Their instinct was to run, but the ground in every direction was covered with hungry crabs headed straight toward them.

Julia started to pass out, so Jack and Conor immediately lifted her over their heads and tried to carry her down toward the beach—if they made it to the water, they'd be saved. But it was a long way.

They were all now completely covered with crabs. The crustaceans instinctively went for the most vulnerable parts of the body. They focused their attacks on the boys' faces: Jack had a crab hanging from his cheek while another bit his lip and tried to crawl into his mouth.

As the boys ran, they stumbled over a boulder. In a last desperate gesture Conor and Jack threw their bodies over Julia, but it was too late. Thousands of red-tipped claws were racing toward them. They would be eaten alive.

"*Mona'a ah mona'a li, 'iya suqa mona'a! Waliya mona'a!*" A shrill voice rang out, speaking an unfamiliar language. It was talking to the crabs.

The clawing and biting abruptly stopped, and the green horde began to retreat.

Conor leapt to his feet, pulled a crab out of his hair, and pulled Jack up by the shoulder. His big brother, covered with scores of tiny wounds, was bleeding profusely from his ear and nose; Conor imagined he looked even worse. Gently, they raised Julia to her feet.

Julia was in a daze. Her face and bare arms were swollen, and they feared she was suffering from toxic shock. She kept mumbling: "Weasel, where is my Weasel?"

In front of them stood an apparition: a young woman, perhaps in her early twenties, with fine noble features, mocha skin, and the fiercest green eyes they had ever seen. She was cradling the wounded but still breathing civet in her arms. She had saved their lives.

Conor thought she looked like an Irish fairy or a medieval angel, but she was a Socotran sorceress, a *zahra*. Her name was Tatra.

CHAPTER FIVE: *Tatra's Story*

One of the villagers told us of the female jinn *who roams the*
mountains at night. "And if you meet one," he said, "she sings to you."
Socotra . . . the Celtic fringe of Arabia.
TIM MACKINTOSH-SMITH [14]

25 . HEALING

*T*atra motioned to the boys to follow her. While Conor carried Julia on his back in a "fireman's hold," Tatra cleared a path through the green horde. The crabs—so ferocious a few minutes earlier—scurried timorously out of the beautiful *zahra's* way.

A few hundred feet ahead was Tatra's house, built on a rugged platform of limestone that projected from the sand like the overturned hull of some ancient ship. Nearby was a huge cairn, thirty feet high; it was unclear whether it was a primitive warning beacon or a monument to one of Ras Momi's infamous shipwreck disasters.

The sorceress lived in surprising comfort. Her stone house with its massive foundations resembled the dwelling of a prosperous crofter (if such a thing existed) in the west of Ireland or the Hebrides. Inside it was furnished with crude but well-made furniture and full of items— canned foods, flashlights, bottled water, perfumes, and most surprisingly, shelves of books—rarely found even in the wealthiest Socotran homes. Tatra obviously had a benefactor.

The boys laid Julia on a bed, and following Tatra's command, they then stretched themselves out on the floor. Starting with Julia, Tatra rapidly and methodically treated their wounds with a balm of dragon's blood resin, rare aloes, and turmeric root. While their hands and faces had been clawed to hamburger, their eyes, fortunately, were undamaged.

Jack, almost in shock himself, remembered a summer long ago when he and his father had traveled to Rome and stayed near the Coliseum. He remembered their guide explaining how wounded gladiators were healed with an exotic ointment of dragon's blood—how ironic to think that now he was such a wounded gladiator.

After attending to their myriad cuts and punctures, Tatra brought out a large bag of *qat*. She showed the boys how to chew it and then store the plug in the hollow of their cheeks; gently cradling Julia's head, she put some in her mouth as well. Julia's face was still grotesquely swollen, and she had great difficulty chewing.

Conor moved to aid Julia, but Tatra brushed him away.

Jack, meanwhile, was amazed at how quickly the combination of balm and *qat* worked to soothe his wounds and relieve his anxiety. While Yemeni poets had spent centuries trying to capture the subtle but profound effects of *qat*, Jack thought that it was almost indescribable: something like a combination of childhood hot chocolate before bedtime and a general anesthetic.

Conor was also feeling the effect, and the disciplined athlete finally yielded to the emotions of the ordeal. He hugged his big brother, tears streaming down his cheeks. In their previous adventures, they'd never faced anything quite as unexpected or horrible as the crabs.

Julia was slowly coming out of shock. The swelling was going down, and she needed to talk.

"How badly hurt am I?" she asked Tatra in Arabic.

"You'll be fine. The balm will heal your wounds, and *qat* will restore your spirit."

"Why did the crabs attack us? I've never seen anything stranger."

"There are far stranger things on Socotra," Tatra answered coldly.

"But the crabs . . ."

Tatra shrugged her shoulders. "The crabs crave the sweet pink meat of men. For thousands of years ships and sailors have died on the reefs of Ras Momi. I suppose the crabs originally ate only the bloated bodies, but now, when they're famished, they don't wait for the sea."

As Julia translated, Jack recalled an account he had read about the destruction of the P&O steamer *Aden* off Ras Momi on a stormy June night in 1897. He shuddered when he thought about the fate of the 138 passengers and crewmen. How many had been consumed by crabs?

This thought made him even more grateful to Tatra for saving their lives, and he asked Conor to thank her. Conor did the best he could in his beginner's Arabic.

The witch was scornful. "Don't thank me, thank her." She pointed to Julia. "If it had just been the two of you, I would've happily let the crabs have their meal."

"But why me?" asked Julia.

"Because we are sisters." Tatra fixed Julia in her powerful gaze. "For weeks I've heard rumors about another *zahra* on the island. I've been hoping that you would pay me a visit."

"Why do you assume that I'm a witch?"

"Why? Because no one in centuries has succeeded in domesticating a civet—obviously you're a *zahra*. In fact, I wouldn't be surprised if that civet isn't one of your enemies or an unfaithful lover bewitched in a spell."[15] Tatra laughed.

Julia felt flattered.

Tatra got up and walked to the far corner of the room. She returned with Weasel and handed him to Julia. While Julia held him, Tatra applied balm to his badly cut-up little body. Poor Weasel whimpered.

Conor, meanwhile, couldn't take his eyes off Tatra. She was simply the most beautiful human being he had ever seen. He had expected to find an old hag, like in a fairy tale, with an eagle beak of a nose and green seaweed for hair. Instead, Tatra was sublime.

But her beauty was also deeply disturbing. In her eyes, those incomparable emerald eyes, there was an unfaltering radiance like sunlight reflected from steel—Conor interpreted it as almost supernatural strength of will. No wonder others feared her.

Conor looked at Jack, who glanced back. He too was transfixed and slightly frightened by Tatra's unexpected majesty.

26. SCREAMING

As the sun set, the wind began to pick up. Tatra securely barred the door of her house with heavy metal latches and lit a kerosene lantern.

The solitary window was a double-glazed porthole framed by gorgeous teak and rosewood—obviously from the wreck of a grand passenger ship. Jack squinted through it and thought he could see figures moving about.

The wind outside was ranting like a Force Five gale on the Irish Sea, but Tatra didn't pay it the slightest attention. Conor, however, walked over to the porthole. Jack was already peering out, and both boys put their ears against the glass.

"Do you hear what I hear?" Conor asked Jack.

"I'm not sure I want to talk about it." Jack was feeling tense again; perhaps he should chew more *qat*.

"Really, Jack, it sounds like people screaming. I mean, there's the wind howling, but inside it, this other sound. This lament. It's downright *skawly*." Conor looked anxiously at his brother.

Jack didn't know what to make of the eerie sound, but he desperately needed a big dose of Conor's usually reliable humor.

"Well, what do you think, bro? Isn't Ras Momi the dream location for a Club Med resort?"

His younger brother sprang back into form. "Aye, especially for single crabs. Lots of charming company and great kip, what with the reliable supply of dead sailors and the odd idiot hikers like us. Five stars."

The brothers backed away from the porthole. Let the damned souls and drowned men scream all they want; Jack and Conor were tired of being spooked. They weren't going to pay any attention.

27. AN IRISH LULLABY

Julia was trying to coax Tatra's story out of her. But Tatra preferred to sing, in a voice so soft that she was barely audible against the background of the wind and the stranger sounds outside. The song, in an odd language that Julia wasn't even sure was Semitic, had the melody of a nursery rhyme. It was unsettling.

"Now you sing," she more or less commanded Julia in Arabic.

"I'm afraid I can't." Julia still felt too ill. "But he can. He has a lovely voice." She pointed to Jack.

Tatra's intense green eyes drilled like lasers into Jack's brain. After a minute she said, "Then sing."

Although Jack was hardly in the mood, it seemed wise to make an effort. He surprised both Julia and Conor by singing in Irish. It was a haunting song, a lullaby actually, from the terrible days of the 1840s. It sent a chill up Julia's spine.

Tatra also seemed moved. She thought for a long moment, then said to Jack: "We too often sing of black famine years and the children we've lost."

Julia translated, then asked Jack, "Is that what you were singing about?" Jack nodded yes and looked at Conor, who was shocked. Tatra knew Irish?

"Come closer." Tatra beckoned for Jack and Conor to pull their chairs next to the bed where she sat with Julia. Perhaps she was changing her opinion about feeding them to the crabs.

Julia again begged Tatra to tell them her story, and this time she obliged.

"My story begins several thousand years ago . . ."

28. TATRA'S TALE

"Do you know who Aristotle was?"

The kids were surprised by the question. "Yes, we've all studied Greek philosophy in our universities," answered Conor.

"Then I also assume you also know about the Macedonian Alexander, the conqueror of Asia."

The kids nodded their assent.

Tatra pulled an ancient book off the shelf. Written in the tenth century, it was a history by the famous Arab savant al-Masudi. She showed a passage to Julia.

"According to al-Masudi," Julia explained to the boys, "it was Alexander's tutor, Aristotle, who convinced him to colonize Socotra, the ancient world's principal source of incense. The Greek expedition, hand-picked by Aristotle from amongst his own townsmen, included some of his students." [16]

"That would have been sometime around 330 B.C., right?" Jack was thinking out loud.

"Yes. And according to this account, the Greek settlers were merchants, sailors, and teachers."

"The ancestors of the *badw*?" asked Conor.

Tatra answered. "In those days, the *badw* lived down on the plains, and each clan tended its own plantation of frankincense and myrrh trees. We dwelled in great communal houses and spoke both Socotri and Greek. Women were powerful."

"What do you mean?" Julia asked.

"Our clans were headed by matriarchs who were priestesses of the moon. Adult women were the full equals of men, and some became poets and singers. They had Greek tutors and read Aristotle and the Elysian mysteries. They traveled widely, to Ethiopia, India, even to Egypt."

"Then what happened?" asked Jack.

"After the collapse of the Classical world but before the rise of Islam, Socotra was invaded by the Mahri tribes from southern Arabia. They were our cousins, I suppose, but they had entirely different ways of life. Their tribes were ruled by men, and women had little or no authority."

Tatra, who had been gently petting Weasel, lowered the sleeping animal to the floor and then resumed her tale.

"From then on, the *badw* were pushed back into the mountains, and our tree plantations were cut down or withered from lack of attention. Only the stone walls survive to taunt us with our former glory. We became poor pastoralists, half-starved goatherds. Our books were destroyed, and we lived in caves like prehistoric people. The Nestorian monks, and later, the Portuguese Jesuits and the Wahabi *imams* persecuted us as witches."

"But weren't you witches?" Conor asked.

Tatra threw back her hair and laughed. "Secretly we clung to our old culture. The teachings of Aristotle were passed down in stories, along with smatterings of Greek and other ancient trading languages. *Badw* women, once so powerful, organized secret sororities. They continued to be healers, singers, magicians, and moon worshippers—they became *zahras.*"

"So witchcraft has been the echo of this former world—the manifestation of female resistance to a succession of patriarchical conquests," said Jack, as Julia struggled to translate his complicated thought.

"Yes," responded Tatra. "But resistance gradually faded in the face of centuries of persecution. My sisters were flung into the sea from high cliffs, walled alive inside caves, burned at the stake, and exiled to lonely deserts. By the time the British left, only one female-headed clan remained. Only a single clan preserved the ancient knowledge, medicines, and songs. The rest of the *badw* forgot; they became sleepwalkers in their own land."

"And this was your clan—the village of Amia." Julia was beginning to understand.

A shadow seemed to cross Tatra's face. "We were driven into the inaccessible cliffs, just sixty of us. Because no one would have anything to do with us, our clan became inbred as we married our own cousins.

There were strange sicknesses. We had few goats and were always hungry. To keep the children alive, our men became pirates. Then the soldiers came, and they destroyed our homes and threw our animals into the sea. They relocated us to a camp on the southern plain."

Tatra stood up, circling behind the boys.

"The local people feared and despised us. They blamed me in particular for every accident and misfortune. If a goat fell into a pothole or a child took a fever, if there was a strange stone in their path or an unfamiliar noise in the night—it was my witchcraft. My cousins feared they would attack us or send us to the mainland, so they denounced me. My own cousins exiled me: I was forced to come here, where no human being would live."

"So you were the head of the clan?" asked Julia.

"There is no more clan. The way of the *zahras* is finished. I eke out my days with crabs and ghosts. I can never marry or have children— the lineage is dead. All that remains of the old world of Socotra is my angry, monstrous brother, Kaitos. And the pale dragons who dwell under the earth."

29. WOMEN INTO DRAGONS

Tatra refused to talk about Kaitos.

"All the world wants to know where Kaitos is, but I say nothing. The Yemenis beat me, then offered me a fortune if I would talk. I laughed at them. Then they sent me here."

"How about the dragons? Can you tell us about the dragons?" begged Julia.

"This is why you came to see me, isn't it? You want to know about dragons. Why? To put them in zoos? To bring ignorant tourists with their cameras to take pictures of them?"

"Well, no . . . not really," Julia stumbled. "We're scientists. We're studying Socotra's caves . . ." Tatra cut her off.

"Well, my dear, if you want to know about the dragons, I'll tell you. But first let me warn you. If the little crabs scared you, then don't go near the dragons' cave." She chuckled. "The crabs are as nothing compared to the terrors of that cave."

She fixed her gaze on each of the kids in turn.

Conor bucked up his courage. "Well, what do the dragons look like?"

"Remember what I said about my sisters being walled alive in caves by ignorant and evil men? Well, as they starved, went mad, and lost their sight, those doomed *zahras* turned themselves into dragons—eyeless dragons with skins as white as moonlight and as soft and slimy as a dead baby's."

Julia gulped, then translated for Jack and Conor.

"So are you really sure you want me to tell you how to find the dragons?" Tatra had a wicked smile.

"Yes, please help us," replied Julia.

Tatra liked the young *zahra*'s determination. "Go by boat, past Ras Qutaynahan; you'll see the ruin of Amia. Two miles east are the highest sea cliffs on Socotra, where you'll see caves. Wait till dusk—you'll hear the beating of wings. Look up and you'll see bats flying out of a huge cave, the dragons' cave."

"But wouldn't it be easier to go overland? Isn't there any entrance into the cave system from the western plateau?" asked Conor.

"No, it's too dangerous. There are only cracks and potholes. This is important: you always want the light behind you. When the dragons come after you—and they will—you must retreat toward the cave mouth. Sunlight burns their skin, so they will not follow. But only enter the cave during the day, never, *never* at night."

"How do we get into the cave? Lower ourselves down from above?" asked Jack.

"Impossible. The cliff overhangs the cave, so you must climb up from the base. There was once a hemp ladder, but I'm sure it is gone. The rock is slippery and almost vertical, but it is the only way to reach the cave."

"Who used the ladder? Who visited the cave, and why?" asked Julia.

"I did, every week since I was a small girl. The spirits of the *zahras* must be appeased. The dragons eat goats, so each time I took a goat as an offering."

"But what have they eaten since you stopped visiting?"

"I don't know." A dark smile passed across Tatra's face. "The dragons must be very, very hungry."

The *qat* induced a deep, dreamless sleep. When the kids woke up the next morning, they were startled to find that most of their wounds had healed overnight.

Julia rushed to a mirror, expecting to find her face still swollen and disfigured, but she saw only a few scabs. She looked like she had been lightly scratched by a pet cat, not half-eaten by carnivorous crabs.

"Julia, you look great. How do you feel?" asked Conor.

"Amazingly fine. How about you?"

"Fit as a fat leprechaun on a toadstool. It's almost as if yesterday's nightmare didn't really happen."

Tatra interrupted. "Eat. Come and eat."

She served them a rich fish stew cooked in a traditional Socotran pot, which was decorated with geometric designs painted in dragon's blood resin; she had also opened the two tins of peaches that were among the gifts brought by the kids. A pot of tea was brewing.

"I was famished, this is brilliant." Conor licked his chops.

Jack was a little mouldy (*qat* hangover, perhaps?) and started with the tea.

"Conor, this is uncanny. Try your tea."

"Umm, same as Mom's. If we weren't three thousand miles from Dublin having breakfast with a witch, I'd say this is a cuppa Bewley's."

Julia tapped Conor on the shoulder. He turned around to find her holding a battered canister of Bewley's Irish Breakfast tea. Everyone laughed, then Julia explained the joke to Tatra.

"Kaitos keeps me well provided with necessities," she explained. She went to the cupboard and returned with three bars of Swiss chocolate, and she gave a bar to each of the kids. Weasel seemed just as delighted to receive some leathery goat's meat, which he devoured with the gusto of a gourmet.

While the boys finished breakfast, Tatra took Julia into a corner. It was obviously a matter of highest urgency.

"Remember I said that there were stranger things to fear than crabs?" she whispered.

"Yes, the dragons . . ."

"No, not the dragons—there is something else: an evil power beyond comprehension. A destroyer of worlds . . ." Tatra began to tremble.

Julia was unnerved. Killer crabs and hungry dragons were quite bad enough. "What is this threat?"

Tatra closed her eyes and brought her fists to her temples. It was as if she were trying to focus a third eye, an eye that could see the future. As she made a fierce effort, every muscle in her face tightened, and Julia could hear her teeth grinding.

"No, it's no use; I can't see clearly. Perhaps there is a gray box with red writing in a strange script." She grasped Julia's hand. "But I can feel the danger. Do you understand? I sense something terrifying."

"Where is it? Is it here on Socotra?"

"Not yet. But it is coming, a poison to kill all of us. It is headed toward this island."

"What can be done?" Julia asked anxiously.

"I can do nothing." Tatra shrugged her shoulders. "I'm watched and cannot leave Ras Momi, so you and your young friends must save Socotra. You alone, Julia, share the power of the *zahras*."

"But how can we stop this evil? Can't you give us a clue?"

"I think if you go to the dragons' cave, the horror will seek you out. And I fear it may have something to do with my brother Kaitos. More I cannot see." Tatra squeezed Julia's hand. "You must be extremely brave."

Tatra kissed Julia gently on the cheek. She took her necklace off and put it around her friend's neck. On a leather cord hung an ancient amulet of the moon.

31. TRINITY

It was time for the team to take their leave. They inspected their gear: while the handheld radio had broken when Julia fell, everything else seemed OK. They still had several days' food, plus the expensive chocolate bars that Kaitos must have liberated from a luxury yacht.

Tatra gave each of them a vial of dragon's blood resin and aloe, with careful instructions on how to use the balm to treat wounds and sores. She permitted each of the boys to kiss her on the cheek.

As Conor opened the door and started outside, Julia grabbed him from behind. "Wait—the crabs," she said anxiously, turning toward Tatra.

"Don't worry, my dear," reassured Tatra, "the crabs won't bother you." She gave Julia a final hug and whispered in her ear. "And remember the urgency of what you must do!"

Julia was tearful. It was difficult to leave the spell of this extraordinary woman who had saved their lives. It was also frightening to be charged with such a strange and awesome responsibility.

The group waved a last goodbye. As soon as they were out of sight of Tatra's house, they broke into a fast walk, then a jog. Only a few timid green crabs were about, but no one was taking any chances.

They jogged until they had regained the sand dunes at the neck of Ras Momi, where they took off their packs off and collapsed. Conor munched on one of Tatra's chocolate bars.

"Julia, what happened? What was Tatra telling you in such secrecy?"

Julia first showed them the amulet that Tatra had given her. It was a naturally moon-shaped pebble of iron or iron-nickel alloy. Jack peered at it closely, then took his Brunton compass from his pocket. He held the amulet next to it.

"Look." The compass needle shifted from true north toward the amulet.

"It's magnetic—I'm almost sure it's a meteorite."

Julia studied it.

"You're right. I'd even make a wild guess that it could be a fragment of the great meteorite in the Kaaba in Mecca. Before Islam and Christianity, many of the tribes of Arabia worshipped the moon. So I guess I am now officially the princess Luna."

The boys laughed.

"Now, tell us what Tatra confided in you," Conor begged.

"OK, here's the eerie part." As Julia related the witch's blurry vision of some approaching apocalypse, she tried to recall Tatra's exact language.

"'Destroyer of worlds?' Why is that phrase so familiar?" Jack was puzzled. Then he remembered.

"'Now I am become death, the Destroyer of Worlds.'"

"What are you raving on about?" laughed Conor.

"Those are the words that Robert Oppenheimer spoke at Trinity in

July 1945. They're from a Hindu scripture."

"Trinity?" asked Conor.

"The first atomic test in the New Mexico desert, Conor. It's about the atomic bomb."

CHAPTER SIX: *Giant Salamanders*

*The land tortoises, crocodiles and giant lizards referred to by the author of the
Periplus have not been found so far, but this is not to say that they did not exist.*
WOLFGANG WRANIK[17]

*The crew ceased talking and stared up at the caves,
as if half-expecting an Arabian Scylla to pop out.*
TIM MACKINTOSH-SMITH, *referring to the southwestern coast of Socotra*[18]

*T*he team knew that Dr. Hasan would be worried by their failure to radio their position, so they decided to return via the north shore. Because here were a number of small villages and even a donkey path supposedly passable with four-wheel drive, they hoped to hitch a ride.

They had only been hiking for about an hour when Conor, who was ahead of the others, ran into Tariq. They embraced warmly, and Jack and Julia soon caught up. Tariq told them that Dr. Hasan, still hobbled by his sprained ankle, was waiting at the village of Sigira just two miles ahead. He had brought one of the Land Rovers.

Thirty minutes later, they had arrived in Sigira and were the center of much curiosity. Most of the locals were shocked, even a little horrified, when Tariq explained that the kids were returning from the tip of Ras Momi.

"Very bad place!" was the consensus. "Home of *jinn* (demons)."

Dr. Hasan, meanwhile, looked as if he, rather than the kids, had been the victim of an ordeal. He was haggard, exhausted, and obviously, much consumed with worry. He was also anxious to get the team away from the village so they could talk frankly amongst themselves.

Thanking the villagers for their hospitality, they headed off in the direction of Hadibo along the wretched coastal road. After about fifteen minutes, they pulled over next to a pretty spring. Jack and Conor amused themselves spelunking in a nearby pothole, while Julia related in Arabic the story of their experiences since the last radio message. Dr. Hasan insisted on every detail, word, and nuance.

"Jack, Conor! Come back. We're ready to meet."

The boys returned. They arranged stones in a circle and sat down. This time the conversation was in English, with Julia translating the highpoints for Tariq in Arabic.

He and Dr. Hasan were in a state of shock from Julia's tale. Indeed, Hasan's initial reaction was to close down the field project and send the kids home.

"This is all my fault. Tariq begged me not to let you go to Ras

Momi, but I dismissed his concerns as superstition. And because of my gross irresponsibility, you were nearly killed. Everything seems to be spinning out of control. There are too many strange plots and subplots. It would be safer just to pack up the project."

The kids argued with their team leader. Jack stressed that the crabs were an explicable but bizarre phenomenon that no one could have foreseen in advance. Julia begged Hasan to continue the expedition to the southwest coast. After talking to Tatra, she was more convinced than ever that some kind of extraordinary fauna survived in the caves. Conor said that as their guide, he, not Dr. Hasan, should be blamed for the close encounter with death.

Hasan reluctantly agreed to go ahead with the expedition.

"OK, we'll keep on schedule: we leave the day after tomorrow. Tonight after dinner we'll do some brainstorming about the 'dragons' and our strategy for exploring the cave. But from now on, safety comes first. If anything unexpected arises, we turn tail and retreat back to base. OK? I need your word on this."

The kids agreed.

"Good. At some point I will talk to the authorities about the green crabs; even if the locals know to avoid Ras Momi, we must ensure that outsiders don't again stumble into that nightmare. We need to get some of the invertebrate biologists back to do a study—I don't know how that was overlooked. Any more questions? OK, then let's go home. I'll play you an old video of the Mets in the World Series."

Everyone laughed and started back to the Land Rover. Suddenly they saw a dust cloud approaching them at high speed.

"What the heck is that?" Jack asked.

Several battered military jeeps pulled up. In the first were two of the red-bereted Special Forces soldiers that Jack and Conor had glimpsed at the airport. In the second were a driver, a Yemeni officer, and a flashback from the recent past: the tall American in Ray-Bans.

"Howdy, partners. Reckoned we'd meet again." Only the American got out of the jeep. This time he was in regulation desert fatigues with a .45 automatic in a shoulder holster.

"Hiya," said Conor without a smile. Jack just nodded.

"And who are you, little lady?"

Before Julia could respond, the cowboy answered his own question. "Well, I guess you must be Miss Julia Monk, honor student from Columbia University. And this distinguished gentleman, I suppose, is Dr. Hasan." The American's eyes narrowed. "Who's the Bedouin?"

Julia was almost breathing fire out of her nose. "This is our colleague and friend, Mr. Tariq al-Qirbi."

"By what authority are you interrogating us?" Dr. Hasan was also angry. "Shouldn't we be talking to that Yemeni officer over there rather than you?"

The Ray-Ban man laughed. "Don't wet your pants, professor. I'm just looking out for your health and safety. I mean, you, the little lady, and Mr. Davis are all carrying U.S. passports, aren't you?"

Hasan didn't answer. Jack noticed the name on the American's uniform: Colonel R. E. L. Strong. He decided to try and change the subject.

"What does 'R. E. L.' stand for, Colonel?"

"Robert E. Lee, son. Robert E. Lee Strong." He gave Jack an evil grin. "Now you answer a question for me. What did you talk about with that witch out there on the point?"

Conor started to say something, but Strong cut him off. "I want Jackson here to answer that."

Jack explained that they were merely seeking information about caves and possible underground fauna.

"Underground fauna. Hmm. That's a funny one." Strong fixed Jack in the powerful unblinking gaze of a professional interrogator.

"Yes, fauna, cave animals, troglodytes," Julia intervened. "We're scientists, as you well know. And we work for the United Nations, which you also know. What else would we be up to?"

"That's the million-dollar question, little lady. But look at it from my perspective: this is Socotra, a notorious base for Arab terrorism. This damn island is a maze of caves. A perfect hiding place for al-Qaeda. And here you are."

Strong pulled a memo from his shirt pocket and began to read it out loud.

"Julia, member of the Green Party, seen at innumerable antiglobalization demonstrations in New York and Washington. Conor, political activities in Dublin unknown, but co-founder of environmental group associated with Inuit extremists in the Arctic. And—this really makes my day—Jack, Caltech student with access to all sorts of advanced military technology. Also some kind of wooly anarchist who doesn't believe—and these are his own words—in 'nation-states or armies.' My, my. Not a very patriotic group, are we?"

"This is enough! I demand you stop right now. You have no authority in Socotra. Let the Yemenis arrest us, or move out of our way and let us go." Dr. Hasan was seething.

Strong walked over and stood a few inches from Hasan's face. The American officer was a good eight inches taller.

"Oh yes," he was still reading from the memo. "Then we have the leader. Palestinian. West Bank, Gaza. Travel in several countries unfriendly to the United States. A naturalized citizen and 'eminent' scientist." Strong laughed sardonically. "Probably a 'sleeper' for Hamas or some other terrorist group."

Dr. Hasan was ready to take a swing at Strong, but Julia grabbed him by the arm. "Ignore him. Let's go, Dr. Hasan." Then she turned to Strong. "We're leaving. If you believe we're terrorists, shoot us. If you think we've committed a crime, arrest us. But otherwise, *adios, amigo.*"

Strong shrugged his huge shoulders. "Shoot you? Perish the thought. Arrest you? Maybe. Keep you under surveillance? You bet your life. If you know what's good for you, you'll come running to me with any information you find out about the terrorist Kaitos. Anything strange in those caves, tell me. Otherwise, we'll continue to assume that you are terrorist sympathizers using the UN as cover. In my book, you're guilty as hell until otherwise proven innocent. Think about that. And have a nice day, y'all."

Strong walked back to his jeep. The Yemenis had remained impassive through the entire exchange. They drove away in another cloud of dust.

34. SECRET WEAPON

The team was fuming in anger.

"I'm up to ninety with that bucket of snots," Conor complained in Dublin slang.

"I know, I feel like I've just been mugged," said Julia. She turned to Dr. Hasan. "But please don't call off the expedition."

"Don't worry, Julia. This little encounter has erased my doubts. We're going to Tatra's cave if only to prove that science has a right to exist on Socotra. I'll also notify the UN as well as the university that we're being harassed. Maybe they can get the Pentagon to call its dogs off."

Tariq looked glum. "What are you thinking?" Jack asked.

"That American *jinn* knows something you don't. Can't you see— he's a big spider spinning a web. He's planning to trap you."

"Maybe so," Jack replied. "But if we run away from Socotra now, he'll have won. We just need to be smarter and faster on our feet than him."

"Plus we have a secret weapon that the Pentagon knows nothing about," added Julia.

"What's that?" asked Conor.

Julia pulled Weasel out of his pouch and held him up. "Super Civet!"

35. WHAT DO THE AMERICANS WANT?

Back in camp, Samira carefully examined the kids' wounds. As a precaution, she gave them tetanus boosters and took blood samples from each of them. She and Julia stayed in the lab to examine the ointment that Tatra had given them while the brothers went off to splash in the pool for an hour.

Dr. Hasan, meanwhile, wrote up a brief report on their encounter with the American. He asked Anwar to take it back to Hadibo that evening for transmission to the main UN field office in San'a. He also asked Anwar to find out what the local rumor mill in Hadibo was saying. Did the Americans actually believe that terrorists were hiding out underground in Socotra? And did the pirate Kaitos actually have some connection to al-Qaeda or other groups? For the kids' safety Dr.

Hasan needed some answers quickly.

Dr. Hasan knew that Socotra had long been a persistent hallucination in the eyes of the CIA. They had spread wild allegations in the late 1970s that the island was a training camp for international terrorist groups such as Black September, the German Red Army Faction, and others. They also publicly claimed that the Soviets had built a huge base on the island for their nuclear submarines.

It turned out that there was no Soviet base at all, just an occasionally used offshore anchorage. And the locals scoffed at the idea of terrorist training camps. "Germans? Palestinians?" Tariq had said skeptically, laughing as if were a preposterous fantasy.

But what the Socotrans did take seriously was Washington's public demand to be allowed to establish an electronic eavesdropping post on the island. After the U.S. destroyer *Cole* was damaged by a terrorist attack in Aden Harbor in October 2000, San'a had come under enormous pressure to give American special forces and intelligence operatives free rein.

Then came the September 11 attacks on New York and Washington. It was well known that Osama bin Laden's family originated in north Yemen and still retained many ties in the region, so at risk of being branded a "terrorist state" themselves, the Yemenis were forced to open the door to secret U.S. military operations. This included Socotra, although San'a was still resisting the demand for formal bases or listening posts.

"What do you think this all means, Anwar? You're the expert," said Hasan.

Anwar had once been a high diplomatic official in the former left-wing government of South Yemen. During the violent civil war that followed unification, he had left for Algeria, where he taught in a university and generally led a comfortable life. However, he was homesick for his native land, and he returned home in the late 1990s. His punishment for his former political views was demotion to his current lowly position in a location that many mainland Yemenis disparaged as the Devil's Island of Arabia.

"Well, Hasan, I hardly think that any of our homegrown pirates are international terrorists. Nor do I believe that occult forces, whether dragons or Mr. bin Laden, are under our feet. But I do worry that the

CIA will stop at nothing to obtain a permanent base on Socotra. 'By hook or by crook,' I believe is the expression in America."

"That sounds ominous. Please explain."

"Well, the classic gambit is to foment or take advantage of some sensational incident. For example, if the United States were to suddenly reveal to a shocked world that a terrorist group had disguised itself as a UN research team."

"You don't really mean that, do you?" Anwar was scaring Dr. Hasan.

"Unfortunately I do, my dear friend. Do you seriously think that the CIA—or for that matter, any competent intelligence agency—would shrink from a little deception if they thought it expedient to accomplish a strategic goal?"

"So you're saying that this Colonel Strong fellow wasn't just bluffing—that they might actually try to frame me and the kids, set us up as 'terrorists?' Oh, come on, Anwar, this sounds far-fetched. We're the UN, for godsakes."

A sad smile crossed Anwar's face. "And what is the UN? I fear, Hasan, that like many men of science you are somewhat naive about *realpolitik*. Believe me, the UN would desert you in a second if they thought the Americans had any evidence of terrorist ties. And 'evidence' is for sale everywhere. I know people who can get it for you wholesale."

Hasan was genuinely shocked. "If that is the case, Anwar, then we have a grave responsibility. What do you advise we do? Should I send the kids home tomorrow and wrap up the research?"

"Would you and Samira leave as well?"

"No, we can't. Not now. Samira is absolutely committed to her well-baby program and won't leave until the end of the summer. I'm serious—she would regard your warning as mere paranoia. There's no way I can convince her to give up such important work. She's saving babies' lives."

"In that case, we must proceed discreetly. Give me a few days to contact some old friends on the mainland and see what I can find out about the CIA's game on Socotra. Go ahead with your expedition. When you return, I should have enough information for us to make an informed decision about closing down the project or not. But do be careful, old man. Something sinister is afoot."

Anwar shook Hasan's hand and began his drive down the mountain.

This evening he had something more serious to worry about than the local vampires.

36. THE HUMAN FISH

Hasan didn't mention his conversation with Anwar to the kids. He figured what they all needed for a change was some science, good old-fashioned science. It was, after all, the reason they were on Socotra, not to be part of some convoluted and treacherous war game.

He asked Julia to present her hypothesis about possible cave megafauna. Everyone was quite excited to hear her ideas, and Samira attended, as well as Tariq and one of the older kids from the village whom Conor had already singled out as a future eco-guide.

Julia spoke outside against the background of a clear, star-studded sky. She unleashed Weasel so he could chase chameleons, his favorite *hors d'oeuvres*. She illustrated the talk with slides projected onto the clinic wall from her laptop. The first slide was a photograph of *Proteus anguinus*. Weasel looked up at the image and blinked.

"Who knows what this is?"

"Bizarre. The translucent body looks like an eel, but it has tiny legs and arms. And the pink head looks almost like a baby's." Samira was slightly revulsed.

"Yes," added Tariq, "it looks like a strange little man. Perhaps a *jinn* made by a *zahra*?"

"In fact, local villagers still call it the 'human fish,'" Julia explained. "Otherwise, it is usually known as an 'olm.' It's about a foot long and lives only in a few limestone caverns in Slovenia and neighboring parts of Italy and Croatia."

"But what the heck is it?" Jack was still confused.

"A neotonic salamander, like the Mexican *axolotl*, that lives like a fish. Except this one dwells in deep subterranean waters in complete darkness. Like other cave-adapted animals, it has compensated for its loss of sight by the extraordinary development of its other senses. For example, its inner ear is fantastically sensitive, and not just to sound: it seems to have the ability to orient itself to magnetic fields, even extremely weak ones."

"Is it completely without optic nerves then?" Samira asked.

"Not exactly. Although its eyes have atrophied, the dermal melanophores in its skin are acutely sensitive to light. If suddenly exposed to sunlight, it might die, literally burn to death. Also, its pineal gland retains some optic, 'third-eye' function, although this is not really understood."

"How about its metabolism?" Dr. Hasan queried.

"A typical troglodyte, it lives in slow motion. It takes seven or eight years to sexually mature and can live for at least eighty, but perhaps more than one hundred years. It can go weeks without food."

"So it's in semi-hibernation most of the time?" asked Jack.

"Yes, except this doesn't seem to affect its reflexes. Like other amphibians, it has extremely fast reactions, even starting from a hibernated or dormant state."

"What does it eat?" asked Tariq, a little nervously.

"Mainly insect larvae, along with the occasional mollusk or worm . . . whatever it can find. Cave dwellers can't afford to be picky eaters."

"OK, Julia," Conor was thinking out loud. "So the existence of the olm provides reasonable grounds for speculating that blind salamanders might survive in other cave systems. 'Wrecks of former worlds' is, I believe, Darwin's phrase for troglodytes. But the olm is small and looks like a snake or a fish—hardly the 'dragon' of Socotran legend."

"Good point, but look at my next slide." Julia now showed *Andrias davidianus*.

Tariq gasped and Jack rubbed his eyes.

"What in the heck is THAT?" Samira exclaimed.

"Godzilla?" offered Jack.

"Japanese giant salamander?" suggested Conor.

"Close—its larger Chinese cousin, *davidianus*. Welcome to the Permian epoch." (Hasan explained to Tariq and the young villager that Julia was referring to the period of earth history when giant amphibians ruled on land.)

"How big?" asked Jack.

"The record is more than two meters, or 6.6 feet long."

"Jappers!" Conor was awed. "Practically a crocodile."

"But no one really knows how big they can grow. They're nocturnal and extremely reclusive. They live in muddy crevices or holes in the banks of cold, fast-moving mountain streams throughout southern China. They eat fish, snakes, water rats, turtles, crabs—you name it. Anything that tries to swim by. They've incredibly powerful jaws and could easily bite your arm off."

"Now, this really looks like a dragon." Dr. Hasan was impressed. "So let's do a thought experiment. Thanks to the Belgians, we now know there are many underground streams and rivers. Some of them have fish, and at least the shallower parts of the caves have lots of freshwater crabs. Not to mention goats—the *badw* are always complaining about how many goats disappear into sinkholes or caves."

Julia was pleased. "Well, Dr. Hasan, you've more or less finished my argument for me. The riparian cave habitats should be capable of supporting something between the size of an olm and the *Andrias*."

"But wait, Julia." Conor thought he had found a weak link in Julia's argument. "That's not your entire hypothesis. You are also claiming that this unknown blind species has evolved over the last two thousand years from its terrestrial ancestors, the ones described as 'lizards' in the *Periplus*. Isn't that right?"

Julia nodded.

"Isn't that an extraordinary short time span for speciation to take place?" Conor was speaking on behalf of Darwinian orthodoxy.

"Sure, most textbooks of evolutionary biology would say that. But we've recently discovered species of fish, even birds, that have become distinct species in even shorter historical periods. Why not an amphibian? My real point is this: if we did find blind salamanders, it would have major theoretical repercussions. Major."

"I agree, Julia, it certainly would. Even though I remain skeptical that they actually exist, this is a really exciting hypothesis. So let's go get 'em—right, Weasel?" Conor offered Julia's pet a piece of kebab. He nearly took Conor's finger as well.

After a few more minutes of informal star-gazing, everyone headed for bed.

Jack stayed up to fiddle with the frequency on the electronic beacon he had installed on the roof of the clinic. Part of his research project for Caltech was to determine if his little MAVs had the ability to home in on weak radio signals. While Jack suspected that this might have potential military applications, he still planned to release one of his bats from the cave the day after tomorrow. Then he would decide whether to report the experiment or not.

Dr. Hasan, for his part, was delighted with the evening. Julia had really strutted her stuff, and now they were back on the track of science. He slept soundly despite his anxieties about the Americans.

Conor, on the other hand, tossed and turned all night long. He kept dreaming that he was being chased through a labyrinth by giant salamanders. When he finally found a way to escape, there, blocking his path, was Robert E. Lee Strong in his dark glasses.

37. RECONAISSANCE

Anwar had arranged for the little expedition—the kids plus Dr. Hasan—to borrow one of the boats that the UN marine biologists had used for their reef research the previous year. It was a twenty-eight-foot, outboard-powered, center-console fishing boat with the dreamy name *Aladdin.* Except for the high-performance boats used by the pirates, it was probably as fast as any vessel on the island. Everyone felt they were traveling in style.

The group left camp before dawn, and by mid-afternoon they were riding the chop off Ras Shaab, the westernmost point on Socotra. Julia and Conor sat watch on the bow, transfixed by the abundance of stingrays, sharks, and large sea turtles. Now and then they also spotted one of the sinisterly graceful and poisonous sea snakes that are common in the Gulf of Aden—it was definitely not a good idea to fall into the water.

Their plan was to land at Tatra's abandoned village, Amia, and set up camp before dusk. They then hoped to go back out to sea and look for the telltale flight of bats leaving a cliff-face cave.

The ruins of Amia consisted of half a dozen roofless mud huts perched sixty feet above a tiny cobbled beach. It was forlorn but well protected. There was a narrow path, but it was so steep and slippery that Conor went ahead of the others to hammer in a few pitons and string some rope for a hand guide. With his still-swollen ankle, Dr. Hasan had an especially hard time.

The village had obviously depended almost entirely on the sea, although there were a few tiny garden plots. There was also a hair-raising trail zigzagging six hundred feet to the top of the cliff; ancient goat droppings signaled its former purpose.

"I get vertigo just looking at that trail. Do you suppose they actually herded goats up and down it? If you slipped, you fall the height of the Chrysler Building to the sea." Julia was flabbergasted to imagine Tatra as a young girl hiking the side of the sheer cliff every morning.

Conor walked to the top so he could scout the plateau beyond. He came down a half hour later.

"That was a cheap thrill. In some areas the trail isn't more than fourteen inches wide; I had to use handholds. There's an arrete that connects to the Western Plateau. I still think it might be better to attempt the cave from the top."

"But remember what Tatra said about the overhang," said Jack.

"Yeah, I suppose she knows what's she talking about."

They tidied up one of the ruined huts and left their sleeping bags and cooking equipment inside. Then they climbed back down the cliff and boarded the *Aladdin*.

Fifteen minutes and about two miles later, they were anchored off the highest sea cliffs on the island. They had expected to see a couple of caves, but in fact, the 1,600-foot-high cliff face was honeycombed with openings of all sizes. The limestone here had a yellowish hue, and the setting sun gave the cliffs a strange jaundiced glow.

It was creepy, and it reminded Jack of a singularly sinister place in Greenland where Conor and his friend Qav had nearly been killed by a calving iceberg.

"Remember Puisortoq?" he whispered to Julia and Conor.

"Shhh!" said Conor. "I'm superstitious."

"Me too," added Julia, uncharacteristically.

The sun sank into the sea as if into a pool of blood.

"Beautiful," said Dr. Hasan.

"Eerie," replied Julia.

"Julia, I don't think I've ever seen you so nervous. This expedition is your idea: you should be delighted we're here."

"Sorry, Dr. Hasan. I *am* thrilled that we're finally here, but I just find something upsetting. Maybe it's the corpselike pallor of the cliffs or the blood-stained ocean. I don't know what's spooking me."

Jack put his arm around her. "Probably nothing more than the fact that you were almost eaten alive by crabs two days ago. My god, Julia, you don't have to play super-scientist all the time. I mean, you nearly died on Ras Momi. You're recovering from a near-death experience."

"Me too." Conor squeezed Julia's arm. "I am thinking of serious psychotherapy when I get back home."

"Yeah, probably in McGraw's Pub." Jack playfully pushed his little brother away, and Julia laughed.

They watched the caves for any sign of movement. Julia half expected to see a legendary *roc*, the giant man-eating bird that attacked Sinbad when he sailed by Socotra.

Then, they heard the sound. It began like the rustling of leaves in the dark, then grew steadily in volume until it sounded more like an approaching Boeing 747.

"My god," Dr. Hasan gasped.

From the highest of the cave openings, far under a large overhang—just as Tatra had described it—an immense flight of bats was taking to the sky. There were thousands of the native Socotran mousetails (*Rhinopoma hardwickei*).

"I've never heard bats make a sound that loud," said Jack, awed. At last they were dealing with animals he knew something about. "But then again, I've never seen so many bats at once."

"They're the only truly indigenous mammals on the island," said Julia, her anxiety now replaced by wonder.

"The cave system must be huge, don't you think?" marveled Conor.

The long black stream of bats angled toward the moon, eclipsed it, then turned slowly along the coast and back toward the southern coastal plain.

Conor was thinking about Socotra's infinities of nagging flies, mosquitoes, and fleas, and calculating how much more infernal it would be without the nightly raid of the insectivorous bats. "Go get them, boys," he said to himself.

"Conor, what do you think?" Dr. Hasan snapped him out of his reverie.

Conor carefully assessed the cliff face with a pair of powerful night-vision binoculars; he then drew a rough sketch on a notepad and wrote down some numbers. He seemed mainly concerned with the overhanging roof of the cave itself.

"Well, better limestone than sandstone, although I'd prefer granite. I'd say there's probably an easy 5.8 route from the bottom, a handful of 5.9 pitches, and one pumpy 5.13 over the roof of the cave; the last should be a bit of fun. We'll know for sure in the morning."

"How hard is that?" Hasan asked. He didn't have a clue what Conor was talking about.

"Well, technical enough for us, although I am sure the kids from Terbec could skinny up it in a flash."

Hasan chuckled. "Explain more. Remember, my game's baseball, not rock climbing."

Jack spoke instead. "It's very high, with extreme exposure but with a wealth of holds and safe anchor points. Conor has been climbing sea cliffs like this since he was thirteen; it'll be a breeze for him. Julia might be able to lead it as well. I'm rusty and out of shape, but I could follow."

"It's simple then. We'll let Conor and Julia be the climbing party, while you and I will be the boat crew. Is that OK with you, Julia?"

"Great. I can't wait to get up there. Anyway, I've always wanted a date with Conor." Julia kicked Jack's brother in the shin, while Conor, to everyone's surprise, blushed once again.

38. JULIA'S DREAM

The night became colder, and the moon rose higher; it cast its searchlight over the sea in front of Amia, where Kaitos, the terror of Socotra, had grown up. Large graceful shapes occasionally erupted from the water in low arcs, then splashed back down again.

"Dolphins playing in the moonlight. In Socotran folklore it is a good sign," Dr. Hasan mused.

"Well, after the last week, we could certainly use a change of luck," laughed Conor.

They'd worked out what all considered a fail-safe plan of operation.

Considering Tatra's warning about the aggressiveness of the "dragons," they decided to use Jack's microbats for initial exploration. The problem was that they needed a more stable platform for the microwave transmitter than the rolling deck of the boat.

"What if we set up the transmitter in the mouth of the cave?" asked Conor.

"Probably the only feasible solution," said Jack.

"Easy enough, then. Julia and I will climb up and establish a fixed line. We can then haul up the gear, assemble it, and you can use wireless to control the launch from the boat."

"Wouldn't it be simpler for me to climb up there with you?" Jack asked.

"I dunno; I hate risking your laptop on the cliff. Anyway, we need to see if we can remote control the whole shebang. Why don't we give it a try this way, and if there's a problem, you come up."

Julia piped up. "Also, I think, in case of an emergency, it is always better to be in pairs. If there was a problem with the boat, I'd prefer you to be there with Dr. Hasan. You've had a lot more experience."

"OK, that's fine. But next time I get to go up—I'm dying to see the cave firsthand. Besides, I get along famously with bats." Jack grinned.

They curled up in their sleeping bags. Tonight it was Julia's turn to have a bad dream.

She dreamt that Tatra was standing on the very end of Ras Momi, facing the angry sea with her hands raised above her head. But the *zahra* had only one eye, a huge green eye in the middle of her forehead. In this cyclopean eye Julia could see a reflection of fire. She turned from Tatra and looked to the east. The horizon was a biblical wall of flame to the top of the sky. It was moving toward Socotra, boiling the sea as it came. Behind Julia, Tatra was singing an eerie lullaby.

CHAPTER SEVEN: *Pandora's Box*

The Russian military has lost track of more than
100 suitcase-sized one-kiloton nuclear bombs, said former
Russian national security advisor Alexander Lebed.
60 MINUTES (1997) [19]

Criminal elements in Russia may be poised to
sell nuclear weapons to the highest bidder . . .
ABC NEWS (1999) [20]

*T*here was a loud argument on the ship's bridge. At sea no one is supposed to dispute a captain's judgment in front of his own crew, but the Russian passengers aboard were playing by their own rude rules.

"Damn it, I said leave the lights off." A stocky, tough-looking man in a leather jacket was speaking in English. He had a grayish crewcut and was missing two fingers on his left hand. Everyone called him Semion, but it wasn't his real name.

"But we're only sixty miles from Ras Momi. These waters around Socotra are pirate-infested. Lighting up the ship is standard procedure." The captain, a Greek Cypriot, was appalled by the brutal manner of the Russians.

"Pirates? You think we're worried about pirates?" Semion scoffed. "Vahtang, come here."

Vahtang, the other Russian, was a giant, almost seven feet tall. His face was creased by a deep diagonal scar, as if someone had once attacked him with an axe or meat cleaver. He carried an American MAC-10 submachine gun.

"Vahtang, the captain is worried about pirates. What do you think?"

Vahtang just grinned hideously. His steel false teeth had been filed down to vicious-looking points.

"You see, Captain, Vahtang eats pirates for breakfast. Keep the lights off. I worry about the American navy, not some Arab scum."

"Well, you leased the ship, so we'll do as you say. But for the safety of my crew, please post your other men on the stern."

"If it makes you happy, Captain. Vahtang, go below and relieve Vladimir and Oleg, send them aft, and tell them to blast anything they see in the water. I don't care if it's a mermaid or a fishing boat—destroy it."

Vahtang smiled and went below.

The M/V *Tiraeus* was an old 18,000-ton multipurpose carrier with as much rust as paint above the waterline; no one even dared imagine what the rest of the hull might look like. It was long overdue for the wreckers' yard, but its owner—a reclusive billionaire who lived in Monaco—found it the most profitable vessel in a large fleet that included supertankers and Mediterranean cruise ships. He leased the *Tiraeus* to a single customer: the notorious Sointsevskaya crime family in Moscow.

This most powerful of "Russian mafia" families had employed the *Tiraeus* for the past few years to smuggle a staggering variety of illegal commodities, including heroin, weapons, stolen automobiles, counterfeit U.S. currency, hijacked caviar, industrial diamonds, and undocumented Chinese immigrants. This was the final trip, with the most precious and mysterious cargo: a billion-dollar cargo, in fact.

Locked below in a passenger cabin—and guarded twenty-four hours per day by at least one of the Russians—were two aluminum attaché cases that looked identical to the cases that photographers use to carry lenses and cameras. They were stored in a lead-lined chest. Only the captain and the chief mate had seen the Russians bring them aboard in Vladivostok three weeks earlier.

The ship's manifest, meanwhile, listed a mixed cargo, and indeed, the holds were full of lumber, canned salmon, and vodka. The official destinations were Haifa, Israel, and Nicosia, Cyprus. In fact, the *Tiraeus* was headed for a secret rendezvous near Mayyum Island at the entrance to the Red Sea.

The captain tried to make small talk with the Russian. "Your tattoo, Semion, is that from the Red Army? Afghanistan, perhaps?" He pointed at the symbol of a skull and dagger.

"No, *cher capitaine*," Semion laughed. "It's from the French Foreign Legion. I defected from a Russian trawler in the late 1970s in Marseilles. I joined the Foreign Legion, then after that I worked for the Americans for awhile. Killed a lot of people. Finally, I got a good day job with our business associates in Moscow."

"The others?"

"Vladimir worked for the Americans as well; Oleg is a former Russian paratrooper. Vahtang is just a monster. He was in prison for murdering his family or something. The Sointsevskayas bribed the minister of justice to get him out. I'm the only one he takes orders from. Without me he'd probably murder your entire crew in their sleep."

The captain was sick of Semion's sinister humor. This group of Russians was by far the worst he had ever had to deal with.

There was a sharp jolt, then muffled sounds.

"Did you feel that?" the first mate anxiously asked the captain in Greek.

The captain went to the window of the bridge. There was a commotion on the deck. Suddenly tracer rounds and the sparks from ricochets illuminated a full-fledged gun battle taking place.

The captain turned to give an order. He opened his mouth but never spoke: the window behind him exploded, and he slumped to the floor, shot dead.

Submachine gunfire was soon followed by a shoulder-launched rocket. The bridge erupted in flames. The first mate was gravely wounded and another crewman killed.

Semion, however, was already racing below to the cabin where the mysterious cargo was kept. He found Vahtang in a defensive crouch, pointing his MAC-10.

"Quick, unlock the cabin. We must get off the ship," Semion barked.

Vahtang opened the door as Semion quickly dialed the combination on the lock and opened the chest. He grabbed the two cases, which were surprisingly heavy for their size. "You go first—kill anything that moves. I'll be right behind you. We're headed for the No. 2 lifeboat."

They crossed over to the starboard side of the compartment and then descended two levels to a door that opened onto the poop deck. They had almost reached the door when a pirate burst through it. Vahtang killed him with a long burst from his weapon, then he and Semion ran out on the deck.

The first thing they saw on deck was Vladimir sprawled in a dead embrace with another pirate. The last thing they saw was the tall Somali in a Oakland Raiders T-shirt. He fired his AK-47 until he had emptied the entire clip. The whole ship shuddered when Vahtang's huge body hit the deck.

40. "DESTROY IT!"

The fast attack submarine USS *Seawolf* (SSN 21) was lurking one hundred and fifty miles away, directly in the projected path of the *Tiraeus*.

"I don't understand this at all, Captain. The *Tiraeus* seems to be veering off course. And look at this: I can't quite make it out, sir, but it

could be a small boat following the *Tiraeus* or even moored to it." A young red-headed crewman was intently focused on his monitor screen.

"A pirate attack?" The speaker was a civilian standing next to the captain. He was wearing a jogging suit with a Georgetown logo.

"Or maybe a lifeboat?" The captain bent closer to the infrared image being downlinked from a surveillance satellite.

"Should we make course for the *Tiraeus*?" The *Seawolf's* captain, like that of the *Tiraeus*, was deferring to a powerful and mysterious passenger.

"No. Radio our operatives aboard."

The captain gave an order to another crewman. Several minutes passed.

"No response, Captain."

Everyone looked at the civilian. His face was grim.

"Notify Hadibo, have them scramble the Black Hawks. Code Red. Urgent. Captain, can we talk in private?"

The skipper of the *Seawolf* took the civilian into the code room of the submarine's control and attack center.

"Captain, I want you to take out the *Tiraeus* with a cruise missile. Order the launch immediately. If there is a pirate attack in progress, we can't allow them to seize the cargo. Do you understand? This is a matter of utmost importance to national security."

"But there's a crew aboard the *Tiraeus*." The captain was genuinely horrified by the order. "Certainly they aren't terrorists . . ."

"No time for debate. The operation has been compromised, and our assets may be dead. Sink the *Tiraeus*. The Agency takes full responsibility—as you know, we have full Presidential authorization."

The captain shook his head. "What the hell cargo can that old tramp be carrying?"

"Bait, Captain, bait for the Devil himself. But we can't allow it to fall into the hands of a third party. Attack the *Tiraeus* now and obliterate it."

The captain dutifully had the bosun sound battle stations. The crew was well drilled, and it took less than five minutes to launch two Tomahawk cruise missiles from its bow. A minute later, the *Tiraeus* disappeared forever from the screen. The tiny yellow dot, however, was getting away. It was traveling too fast to provide the *Seawolf* with a clean shot.

The civilian was vexed. "I wish we had fighters aloft. Captain, radio Delta Force again. The Black Hawks have to intercept that little boat. We have to be sure we haven't just opened Pandora's Box."

Conor was in his natural element: he was leading a route on one thousand feet of vertical rock with the sea pounding far below. He would've liked to make it seem heroic, but this cliff was easy as rock walls go, with an almost embarrassing abundance of pockets and holds. And Socotran limestone gave magnificent traction.

Occasionally he found old wooden spikes embedded in the rock and tattered bits of the rope ladder that Tatra had described. Even with the ladder it was hard to imagine the young Tatra ascending this wall, with a goat kid under one arm for sacrifice to the dragons.

He made sure to rig plenty of protection for Julia, who was thirty feet below. Ordinarily a graceful, strong climber, she was having difficulty this morning, so he slowed down, encouraging her to take her time. She was obviously still suffering from the aftereffects of Ras Momi.

When they reached the cave—assuming they weren't immediately devoured by giant hungry salamanders—Conor had one last long pitch of truly challenging climbing in order to put a piton on the outside of the overhang. This would be the pulley fulcrum for the haul rope used to bring gear up to the cave. Treacherous wave-pounded rocks prevented the *Aladdin* from approaching too close to the base of the sea cliff, so they needed a hang point as far out as possible.

Because of the height of the cave they would have to use their climbing line as well as all their spare rope. They should have brought more rope from Dublin, but no one had told him that there were sea cliffs this high on Socotra. Moreover, three-hundred-foot coils of static climbing rope were very expensive, and Conor had borrowed every bit of line that his friends and the university climbing club could spare.

So he reminded himself to be extra cautious with the rope: if for any reason the piton gave way or the rope were cut, he and Julia would be marooned in the cave. And that would be a serious bit of bother.

Jack was having the same apprehensions about the rope as he watched their progress through his binoculars. Dr. Hasan was nervously pacing back and forth on the deck.

"This is too dangerous, Jack. I should never have allowed Conor and Julia to go up."

Jack chuckled. "Not really, Doctor. Conor could probably do this in his sleep with one hand tied behind him. You should see him scamper up sea stacks in Donegal or the ice cliffs in East Greenland. He's even pioneered a new 5.14 route on the Old Man of Hoy in the Orkneys; it's the premier sea cliff in Europe. Believe me, if there were cause to worry, I would—after all, he's my kid brother. But just look at the little beggar climb."

Jack was incredibly proud of Conor.

Dr. Hasan had to admit that it was like watching a professional dancer at work. There was never a wasted or uncertain move, just perfect, fluid, acrobatic motion. It reminded him of Bobby Jones's pitching, or better, the way Mike Piazza suavely leaned into a homer. (Everything in Dr. Hasan's world seemed to be a "Met"-aphor.)

"So Conor must be one of the top climbers in Ireland." Dr. Hasan was trying to calm himself.

"Maybe in all of Europe. His footwork is magic. He can steep-edge or cobble like nobody in the business. But he's not a kamikaze; Conor has a great reputation for climbing safely. He never free solos, cuts corners on protection, or takes stupid risks. Look, they're almost to the cave."

Conor was actually about fifteen feet below on a pitch made rather icky because of the vast quantity of acrid-smelling bat guano plastered to the cliff face. He belayed Julia from a small ledge and waited for her to climb up.

"Phew, this is foul!" she complained. The sharp smell of ammonia was overwhelming. "Sorry, Conor, I don't know what's wrong with me today. You'd think I was just another yuppie gym climber and not an experienced mountaineer."

"Julia, save it." Conor shook his head. "After what you've been through, you should still be in bed with your teddy bear, not a thousand feet up a sea cliff. Just take it slow and easy."

Conor swung out into space to make way for Julia on the ledge. He continued to hang there, high above the water, while he talked to Jack on the walkie-talkie.

"OK, Jack, smooth sailing. This pocketed limestone is lovely, and we're not at all pumped. But the bat dung up here is very nasty indeed. Just remember, they're your little friends, not mine. I'll call again in a minute."

"Julia, come meet the dragons," Conor invited.

"Anything to get out of this toilet." They mantled themselves up to the mouth of cave.

It was, in a sense, disappointing. Nothing was waiting for them— no albino giant salamanders, no bleached bones of previous explorers, just a huge two-hundred-by-sixty-foot opening. Inside, everything was white: more bat guano, precious tons of the stuff. Perhaps this adventure was not going to turn out quite like they had expected.

Conor climbed out to the side of the cave and hammered in several pitons to establish a fail-safe belay.

"OK, Julia, you belay me from here. If the dragons lurch out of the darkness, just pendulum out here on the cliff face. They can't follow."

"Gotcha. But be careful, Conor." Julia looked up.

Despite her own considerable rock-climbing experience, she had no idea how Conor was going to conquer the huge overhanging roof. It was sixty feet above their heads and extended at least fifty feet outward.

"Can you really do that?" asked Julia.

Conor just chalked his hands and smiled modestly.

Back on the boat, Jack realized that the moment of truth had arrived. "Dr. Hasan, don't hide your eyes. Conor's tackling the roof overhang. This is the exciting part."

From below he looked like a human fly. Within a few minutes he was hanging under the roof, defying gravity with some clever fist jams, figure fours, and heel hooks. Hasan gasped and averted his eyes.

But Conor was having a ball. Upside down, he felt like Spiderman. He came out of a bat hang and transitioned smoothly to an Egyptian. Now he was at the lip of the roof and there was a solid line of protection behind him. Curling over the lip would be the *pièce d'résistance*.

He reached over the edge and found a good pocket. "A bomber," he said to himself. He inserted a spring-loaded cam and attached a quick draw. "This will hold an elephant." He drew the webbing tight around his right hand and then calmly let the rest of his body drop free. He had practiced this in the gym hundreds of times.

"Oh my God!" exclaimed Hasan. Conor was dangling by one hand from the edge of the overhang. He was higher than the Empire State Building. Hasan felt faint.

Jack put his arm on Hasan's shoulder.

"It's a classic move, honest. A modified powerglide, a real super-dyno." Jack was so excited he forgot that Hasan didn't understand climbing slang. "Not quite a double mo, but dramatic nonetheless. Conor knows exactly what he's doing. Watch what comes next. This takes incredible strength."

Conor gently swung his lower body back and forth, then he erupted upwards, grasping hold of a protruding knob of limestone with his left hand. Without stopping, he smoothly brought his right leg up and found traction. He now reached for a new, higher hold with his right hand. He straightened the right leg and the left followed. He was standing once again face to face with the cliff. Although he actually had secure footing on a large flake of rock, it looked from the boat as if he were standing on thin air.

Conor, who knew he had delighted Jack with that last move, whistled as he pounded a piton into the limestone. He was an old-school clean climber and didn't like defacing rock with pitons and bolts, but sometimes there was no choice. He clipped another quick draw through the piton, hung a Petzl pulley from it, threaded rope through the pulley, then clipped on to it. Mission accomplished.

He toyed briefly with the idea of finishing the short climb to the top. He could leave a length of fixed rope—it would be handy to have an alternative escape route, but then they might be short of rope for the haul. It was frustrating.

Conor retraced his route. The top belay allowed him to move rapidly along the underside of the roof, an almost horizontal rappel. He soon rejoined Julia, who had covered her mouth and nose with a bandanna.

"Fantastic pitch, Conor," she complimented him. "I'll join your fan club. But let's hurry and haul the gear up. I am suffocating from the smell of defecated insects."

"Yeah, it does remind me of Jack's dirty socks." He grinned as he took off his helmet.

As it turned out, they had barely enough rope to hang the haul line. Moreover, the cave was so high that it took twenty minutes of hard work for Julia and Conor to winch up each load of gear from below. Climbing up seemed easier.

Jack knew they'd be thirsty and hungry, so he'd sent up their packs first, along with some night goggles and flashlights so they could explore a little further into the cave. Next he'd sent Weasel, snarling and upset, in a small cage, followed by some photographic equipment, as well as scuba gear in case they confronted underground water.

Next he planned to send up the heavier microwave equipment. He and Dr. Hasan were too preoccupied with the haul to pay any attention to the sea around them, so it was Julia who saw the pirates first.

"Conor, what's that? Quick, give me your binoculars."

A large, sleek powerboat was moving at high speed from the direction of Amia. With a catamaran racing hull and two-thirds of it out of the water, it looked like it was about to take off and fly. Julia remembered a family vacation to the Florida Keys years before—in Florida, only very rich people and drug smugglers had boats like that.

She got on the walkie-talkie. "Jack, there's a big speedboat headed straight at you. It may be pirates."

Looking through his own binoculars, Jack saw the boat bearing down on them. It had a black iodized finish that must have been invisible at night, so it certainly wasn't a group of local sport fishermen.

"Dr. Hasan, I'm afraid we're in a wee spot of trouble."

Hasan grimaced. "Just be calm, Jack; I'll talk to them. We'll give them whatever they want."

Jack looked up at his brother and Julia in the dangerous cave a thousand feet up in the sky. He felt helpless and angry.

The powerboat decelerated. Through the binoculars Jack could see two thin, tall men sitting on the foredeck with automatic rifles. They looked like Somalis. Another man, perhaps a Socotri or Yemeni, was in the cockpit. Behind him, sitting on some sort of divan, was an astonishing figure: an enormous, whalelike mass of a man with no visible arms or legs, just appendages that looked almost like flippers. He was bald and wore a goatee.

"Look, Doctor. Kaitos is paying us a social call." Then Jack called Conor.

"Can you and Julia make out the fat man on the boat?"

"Holy moley, is that Kaitos?" asked Conor.

"Yup, but don't worry. You and Julia just hang tight. Dr. Hasan is going to talk our way out of this. We'll let Kaitos loot our gear or even take the boat. Maybe I can use Tatra as character reference."

"Listen, I can rappel down the cliff in a second . . ."

"And leave Julia? No, don't even think about it. We'll be OK."

The speedboat was now next to the *Aladdin*, and one of the pirates jumped aboard. He didn't even bother to point his rifle, just smiled and turned to tie up the two boats. The second pirate, wearing a Raiders shirt, was less friendly.

"Are you the doctor?" he asked in Arabic.

"Yes, I'm Hasan."

"Good. And which of the *nasranis* is this one?" He pointed to Jack, using the traditional Arabic term for Europeans.

"His name is Jack. He's a science student."

"*Min Amrika?*"

"No, from Ireland."

"Where's that?"

"A small island near England."

The pirate shrugged his shoulders. "Never heard of it. He looks like an *Amriki*. Which one sings? We want the one who sings."

Hasan looked utterly baffled as he translated the pirate's request for Jack. "What does he mean?"

"He wants me, Doctor. Tell him I'm the singer."

The pirate smiled. "Excellent. Now we have what we came for. Get into our boat." He raised his rifle with real menace.

"No, we can't leave our friends behind." Hasan pointed up toward the cave. The pirate squinted and then yelled something to Kaitos in a language Hasan couldn't understand. Kaitos responded with what was clearly an order of some kind.

The first pirate, the smiling one, pulled his AK-47 from his shoulder and looked up at the cave.

Jack screamed "No!" and rushed him. The other pirate knocked him down with the butt of his gun, then stuck its muzzle into Dr. Hasan's face when he tried to aid Jack.

The first pirate aimed straight at the cave, ignorant of the need to compensate his trajectory for the action of gravity.

Conor, meanwhile, was watching all this through the binoculars. "Julia, get back. Get into the cave. Move! They're pointing a rifle at us."

Julia dropped the rope and stumbled backwards. Just then the pirate opened fire from far below. He was thirty feet too low, and chips of limestone exploded harmlessly below the cave. Conor didn't budge an inch.

The pirate in the Raiders shirt yelled abuse at the other, then he stepped over Jack—out cold on the deck—and aimed his rifle at the cliff. He had obvious military experience and carefully adjusted his elevation.

Bullets started zinging all around Conor. A sharp chip of ricocheting rock cut his cheek, and he dropped to his knees. The rope slipped out of his hands and swung out into the void. "Damn it!" he exclaimed. The haul line was now hanging in front of the cliff, an impossible twenty feet beyond reach.

Julia thought Conor had been shot, and she pulled him into the cave. His cheek was bleeding profusely, but it was only a cut. He started to push her away, but she hugged him tight.

"No, Conor!"

Meanwhile, Jack's unconscious body had been hauled aboard the pirate boat and laid at Kaitos's feet. Dr. Hasan had been bound and gagged.

It took these professional looters only five minutes to load all the rest of the expedition's equipment, including Jack's bats, the microwave gear, and Conor's kayak, aboard their speedboat.

Then Kaitos, who had been studying the cliff with his own binoculars, barked a new command, and his men began to pull the haul line down. Dr. Hasan was horrified and struggled futilely with his bonds.

Julia, in the meantime, was trying to get Conor to sit still so she could attend to his cheek, but he insisted on crawling back to the ledge.

"My god, Julia, they're pulling down the rope!"

Julia could tell by the fierce expression in Conor's eyes that he was ready to do something desperate, so she clasped her arms around him.

"Conor, don't even think about it. You can't reach the rope. Leave it, we'll figure something out. Please."

Conor realized that Julia was right, and he also realized that his immediate responsibility was her safety. He peered through the binoculars. Where was Jack? He could see Hasan tied up next to Kaitos, but Jack was nowhere to be seen.

"What have they done with Jack?" Conor started to panic. "What have the bastards done with him? Where's me brother?" Tears were streaming down his face, mixing with the blood from his cut.

Just then Jack staggered to his feet. He was woozy and disoriented, with a first-class migraine (if not a concussion), but he caught a glimpse of Conor high on the cliff, and he waved. Conor yelled and waved back.

The pirate at the wheel grabbed Jack from behind and forced him to his knees. The Raiders fan smiled sarcastically, then fired two full clips into the *Aladdin*'s hull below the waterline. It started sinking immediately.

Conor handed the binoculars to Julia. "Well, we lost the boat, but Jack and Hasan are OK. If the pirates had wanted to kill them, they would've done so by now."

The thought of kidnapping, which would have horrified Conor just a few minutes earlier, now seemed like a miracle. Jack would survive— he was smarter and more resourceful than any pirate. Besides, he had Tatra's blessing to protect him from Kaitos.

With Jack out of imminent danger, Conor began to contemplate their own situation. Unless he could quickly figure out a way to get them off the cliff, he and Julia had no choice but to spend the night in the cave. He remembered Tatra's warning: "Never, never go into the cave at night."

CHAPTER EIGHT: *Kaitos the Pirate*

Down to the day, he had known only humiliation, disdain for his condition,
disgust for his person. Hence, deaf though he was, he enjoyed, like a veritable pope,
the acclamations of that throng, which he hated because he felt that he was hated
by it. What mattered it that his people consisted of a pack of fools, cripples, thieves,
and beggars? It was still his people and he was its sovereign. And he accepted
seriously all this ironical applause, all this derisive respect, with which the
crowd mingled, it must be admitted, a deal of very real fear.
from THE HUNCHBACK OF NOTRE DAME [21]

The sun was slinking away in the west, toward Africa. Seabirds were beginning to shelter in the cliffs. The sky had grown overcast, and the wind flexed its muscles. The weather was changing.

Conor and Julia made a careful inventory of their survival resources:

1. *Food and water, enough for at least a week if sparingly used*
2. *Bivouac bags, mylar ground cloths, and Therm-a-Rest pads*
3. *Climbing harnesses and hardware, but no rope*
4. *Scuba gear with four small "pony" bottles of air*
5. *Some scientific instruments*
6. *A first-aid kit (in which Julia had included Tatra's magic balm)*
7. *A pair of limited-range walkie-talkies*
8. *Carbide miner's cap lamps*
9. *One set of night-vision goggles*
10. *Photo equipment, including battery-powered strobes and flashbulbs*
11. *Weasel*

"Looks to me like we're fine for a few days." Julia was holding Weasel in her arms. "Outside of a helicopter or a few leads of climbing rope, I can't think of anything we're really missing. Oh, maybe a radio or cell phone. But we're not in bad shape—I mean, look at all this gear. So what's our strategy?"

"No point in waiting to be rescued. It should be easier for us to get out of this cave than for Jack and Hasan to escape the pirates, so we've the responsibility to save them."

"Agreed. But what's our plan?"

Conor walked to the edge of the cliff. "One option is to climb down. Amia is close by, but the surf's too rough and the currents are against us; we'd quickly be smashed to smithereens against the cliff. I suppose we could also bivouac near the base of the cliff and hope a boat sees us, but there are no fishing reefs here and most boats skirt the cliffs far at sea. Likely they'd never notice us."

Julia anticipated where Conor's analysis was leading. "I think you're implying that our only option is to repeat your daredevil ascent of the overhang, aren't you?"

"If worse comes to worst. Remember, there's still a piton up there. We could snail our way along using the webbing, quick-draws, and harnesses as protection in lieu of rope. It would be tough, but not at all impossible."

Julia puzzled long and hard over their gear. "Together we just might have enough webbing, etc., to protect one person, but two? I don't see how that could work."

Conor just smiled.

"Oh no you don't, Mr. Macho Man! If you think that I am going to let you free solo a 5.13 route while I'm safely trussed up, you're out of your mind. It's suicidal. No one has ever climbed a roof like this without protection. You're bonkers."

Conor became more serious. "Look, Julia, even if I can't belay myself, I have lots of chocks and hexes for fantastic holds. Anyway, I've already done this route; I know all the moves. It would be a snap to repeat."

Julia shook her head. "No, I've a better idea. Remember when you asked Tatra about other entrances to the cave, and she said there were some cracks and potholes?"

"She also said they were too dangerous to enter."

"But because of the salamanders, which we don't know for sure even exist. And if they do, it isn't certain they are really such a menace. So my proposal is that we explore the cave for a day or two. If we can't find a route out, we'll come back here—either Jack will have escaped by then and brought us help, or we'll try your mad plan."

"Julia, is this just a ploy to hunt for salamanders?"

"No, Conor, of course not!" Tears suddenly welled in Julia's eyes. "I'm just as frantic to rescue Jack and Hasan as you are, but I'm also worried that your fool gallantry might get you killed. Who knows? There may be a way out just around the corner." Julia pointed into the cave.

Conor felt bad for impugning Julia's motives.

"I'm sorry, Julia; I'm a lousy rat. I know you love Jack too." He bit his lip. "Your point is reasonable. We'll spend twenty-four hours looking for another way out. But if we don't find anything by tomorrow at 6 P.M., we turn around and implement Plan B. OK?"

"Agreed." Julia smiled and wiped away a tear.

In the background the sun was becoming bigger and more oblate as it touched the horizon. The sea was turning blood red again. Conor looked up at the dark layer of stratus clouds and wondered whether the moon would ever come out tonight.

He turned back toward the cave, pushed along by a strong wind. If a storm was brewing, he realized that Plan B was a moot point. They would have no choice but to find light in the tunnel.

He put his arm around Julia. "Well, we're committed to the land of darkness now. Let's get going. If we don't get out of the way, we're going to get run over by a half-million bats. I prefer to be eaten by dragons."

Julia put Weasel in his baby sling, shouldered her pack, and picked up one of the haul bags. She remembered the dolphins dancing in the moonlight the night before. It made her optimistic that they would find an escape in the cave.

44. SEA DEMON

Jack's head was still sore but no longer pounding. He realized that if he weren't so upset about Conor and Julia, he'd actually be enjoying the kidnapping. He had never gone this fast on sea before. The boat was cranking more than forty knots. It was exhilarating.

It was also terrifying, because the driver insisted on keeping as close to the cliffs as possible, probably to avoid radar. Jack hoped he knew the location of every submerged rock and reef—one mistake at this speed and nothing bigger than a toothpick would be left of the boat.

They were again approaching Ras Shaami. To their left, the light on the horizon was going out; it would soon be dark. Night, he realized, was the boat's natural element. It was an invisible nocturnal predator, just like a bat.

The driver now swung around to the west and the open sea, increasing his speed by another ten or fifteen knots. They were practically airborne. Somewhere ahead were Socotra's little siblings: the uninhabited islands known as The Brothers.

Jack thought it might be a good moment to attempt a conversation. He had Hasan ask the Socotri driver where Kaitos had bought the boat. "Bought?" he laughed. "Very funny. It belonged to a Saudi prince, number twenty-seven in line to the throne. His family stole all the oil wealth from the Arab people, so we stole his little toy from him. Right out of Aden Harbor in the middle of the night." He turned to see Jack's reaction, then continued.

"Of course, we were chased by patrol boats, but this is fastest speed-boat in world. Did you know that? It can go more than one hundred miles per hour. No one can catch us. Not even American navy."

Jack noticed the small gold plate on the console. "Spectre 36. Championship Performance. Mercury Powered." The boat had been cus-tom built in the States, probably in Florida.

"Magnificent boat," Jack said.

The pirate sighed. "Yes, but it is like a sheik who keeps a big harem, the fun is hardly worth the expense. We are all the time stealing fuel. Ughh! But it is Kaitos's favorite, his beloved."

"Does it have a name?"

The driver was beginning to doubt the intelligence of the captives.

"Of course; all boats have names. It is now called *al-Jinni.*"

"*Sea Demon,*" Jack translated. He laughed inwardly when he thought of all the American skiffs, bass boats, and weekend sailboats with some variation of the word "genie" in their names; their owners clearly didn't understand the word's fearsome connotations in Arabic.

The Raider fan, meanwhile, had been kibitzing the conversation.

Hasan was curious if the pirate actually knew about American foot-ball. Maybe he could break the ice with some old-fashioned sports talk.

"Do you know what your shirt means?" he asked in a friendly voice.

"Of course," the pirate sneered, "*Amriki* pirates. They have very big boats, very fast. They steal from Muslims. I do not like them." He spat into the sea. Definitely not an NFL fan . . .

"Somali pirates," he continued, "only take from infidels and heretics. We are holy warriors."

"And you," Hasan turned to the driver, "are you a *jihadi* as well?"

"No, my friend," he laughed bitterly. "I am just a poor pirate. Kaitos is my cousin. Our clan was persecuted, exiled, and broken up. This boat is our vengeance."

"Do you usually kill your captives?" Hasan asked.

"Always," said the Raider fan. He then turned away in disgust.

"Don't listen to Amir," said the driver. "His brother was killed two days ago; he is understandably very angry. If you help Kaitos, he won't hurt you. He knows the boy singer is favored by his sister."

Hasan translated.

"But then why did Kaitos try to kill my brother and Julia?" Jack was still fuming.

"That was not the intention—Amir got carried away. Kaitos merely wanted to scare them."

"But now they're trapped in a cave with the dragons."

The driver smiled. "My friend, surely you know that the dragons were once witches themselves. They will not harm the young *zahra*. They will just eat the *nasrani* boy."

45. KAITOS'S OFFER

The moon glowed above the cloud layer but was unable to break through. The boat was now fighting real seas. The wind threw tantrums, alternately bursting violently, then suddenly dying down to a mere breeze. The temperamental weather had put everyone slightly on edge, except for Kaitos, who, remarkably, was asleep.

The Raider non-fan blindfolded Jack and Hasan. "We must be near their hideout," Jack speculated.

The boat slowed, then stopped. Jack heard the sound of surf, but not big waves, just a mild lashing of a reef; they were probably entering a lagoon. Indeed, the driver started up the engines again, and they proceeded slowly for another five minutes. Then full stop.

The driver started yelling at someone in another boat or perhaps on shore.

Kaitos woke up and immediately roared an order. The boat bumped into something, but not hard. The Somali pirate nudged Jack and Hasan to stand up. He removed their blindfolds.

The *al-Jinni* was tying up to an old, half-broken concrete pier. Jack guessed it had been built by the British during the Second World War. They had docked on one of the smaller, uninhabited islands in the Socotra archipelago, but Jack had no idea which one.

Two other pirate boats were already docked. The smaller one, perhaps twenty feet long, had "Millennium" stenciled on the back in a jazzy script. It also had an evil-looking machine gun (Jack thought it was an American M-60) mounted on the console. The bigger boat was another huge catamaran-hulled racer like *al-Jinni*. Jack noticed that all were fully equipped with VHS radios, radar, and GPS.

"Kaitos has a first-class fleet," Jack said in faltering Arabic to the Socrati pirate as he helped his captives out of the boat.

Jack couldn't make out his response, so Hasan translated.

"I'm glad you like our boats. Kaitos is always looking for smart young fellows. Maybe he'll let you join us. A short life, perhaps, but always exciting." The pirate chuckled to himself.

Jack couldn't resist fantasizing for a moment what it would be like to be Jim Hawkins in an Arabian version of *Treasure Island*, with Kaitos as Long John Silver. They would prowl the Indian Ocean in these huge, fast powerboats. Then what would Lucy Chen think of him?

"Jack, watch it!" Hasan grabbed his arm just before Jack absently-mindedly crashed into Kaitos, who was waiting in his divan at the end of the pier. A pirate from another boat pushed Jack back.

"Oops, sorry," Jack mumbled.

Kaitos frowned. "This boy is a real dreamer, isn't he?"

"Please, Kaitos," Hasan implored, "you must let us rescue our friends in the cave. The other boy is his brother. We'll do anything you want. Take our equipment—just let us return to the cave."

Kaitos simply nodded. He ignored Hasan and stared at Jack for a long moment.

Jack had never seen a human being as oddly put together as Kaitos. He looked like a mythical chimera, a monstrous pairing of a head and body from unrelated species. The body, of course, was fabulously immense, like a walrus, with sad little stubs of limbs from which fingers and toes seemed to sprout without real hands or feet.

Earlier on the boat, Dr. Hasan had whispered that Kaitos had an extreme case of a congenital disorder called phocomelia ("phoco," Greek for "seal," refers to the attenuated flipperlike limbs seen in the birth defect).

Kaitos's head, on the other hand, looked like it had been stolen from a Greek statue. He had a handsome forehead, magnificent nose, and the determined chin of a classical hero. Like his sister Tatra, he had extraordinary green eyes, except his were more melancholy than fierce. And Kaitos was much younger than Jack had imagined, perhaps only in his late twenties.

Jack continued where Hasan had left off. "Please, Kaitos, take us back to the cave. My brother and our friend Julia are in mortal danger."

"Worry about yourself," Kaitos replied in an oddly mild tone of voice. "For the moment, the little witch can take care of herself and your brother."

"What do you want from us?" Jack asked.

Kaitos again ignored the question and turned to Hasan.

"This boy is a scientist, no? He's very smart?"

Hasan's brain was swimming with confusion, but he tried to be calm. "Yes, he's an outstanding young scientist. He is an expert on robot flying machines, but he also knows much about electronics . . ."

Kaitos cut him off. "Good. And you? You're a doctor, no?"

"Yes, I am a physician and also a research scientist, a kind of chemist. I'm looking for underground water . . ."

Kaitos waved his hand—he wasn't interested. Hasan stopped in midsentence.

The pirate leader spoke now to both of them.

"I have two wounded men and another strangely sick. I want you to treat them. You will then advise me if they can be moved or not. The Americans are hunting us, and we must leave before morning."

"We'd be happy to attend to your men." Hasan pointed to the pile of gear now unloaded from *al-Jinni*. "I have a bag with some instruments and medicines."

"That's not all." Kaitos's voice now had a sinister tone. "After you have looked after my men, I want to show you something mysterious. If you can explain to me its value, I will let you go. If not, I will drown you both in the lagoon."

Jack shuddered.

Kaitos barked an order, and his men quickly carried him away on his divan.

Amir, the Raider, and the older Socotri, who now introduced himself as "Isa," continued to be their inseparable companions. Hasan's medical case was quickly found, and they were ushered along to a nearby building.

Above the entrance to the bunker, or gun emplacement, was the faint outline of an ancient stenciled sign: "Brighton Pavillion." Inside was an abundance of ironic graffiti left behind sixty years earlier by a platoon of lonely Tommies: "Kilroy Was Here," "Help! Send Betty Grable Now," "Blimey, It's Hot! . . ."

The two wounded pirates, laid out on sleeping mats, were tended to by a young boy with a canteen and rag. In the far corner another figure was seated alone, wrapped in a blanket. He was shivering uncontrollably.

Hasan asked, "Isa, do you have any other medicine? Drugs, syringes, bandages?"

Isa nodded. "Yes, we have various medicines. I'll go get them."

Hasan glanced at the strange case in the corner, then turned to Amir. "The two wounded men could bleed to death, so we're going to attend to them first. I need your help, as well as Jack's and the child's." He pointed to the boy, who recoiled in fear.

Amir glared angrily for a moment, then nodded agreement. He took his AK-47 off his shoulder, ejected the clip, laid the rifle on the ground, and rolled up his sleeves.

Hasan had the young boy boil water while Amir and Jack helped him replace the men's primitive tourniquets. After he stopped the bleeding, he administered sulfa drugs and then carefully examined and treated the wounds.

One pirate had been hit in the shoulder; the bullet had passed through cleanly and the bone wasn't broken. "Lucky wound. You'll be fine," Hasan reassured the young pirate, who turned out to be a cousin of Amir's.

The other pirate was in worse shape: a grazing bullet had opened his gut. Although his bowels hadn't been penetrated, his abdominal muscle was sliced open. Although Jack assumed that the pain was probably incredible, the pirate refused to cry or complain. He just stared at Dr. Hasan with desperate eyes.

After administering morphine, the Palestinian doctor worked with speed and dexterity to sterilize, dress, and then suture the horrible gash. With ingenuity he contrived a direct blood transfusion from Amir, who suddenly became more friendly to Hasan and Jack.

"He should also be OK," Hasan told Isa and Amir. "His dressings need frequent changing, and he may require another transfusion. And he can't be moved for several days. This is extremely important."

The two pirates stared impassively without reaction. Hasan feared the implication of their silence, but he realized that argument would be fruitless. They moved on to the third man.

He mumbled that his name was Mohammed, and he was another of Kaitos's cousins. He had been vomiting blood and was extremely weak. He also had a nosebleed and a strange rash on his face. Dr. Hasan examined Mohammed's arms and chest; his skin was inflamed, and his hands and forearms looked like they had been scalded. The sick man gave Hasan a pleading look.

Hasan was puzzled. "Has this man been exposed to acids or caustic chemicals?"

Amir whispered something to Isa. They looked embarrassed.

"Come on, I need an answer," Dr. Hasan insisted. "This man has been poisoned. He is mortally ill. In order to treat him, I need to know what substance he has handled. Sulfuric or nitric acid, right?"

Isa responded. "No chemicals."

"Then what?" Isa and Amir looked at their feet.

"The Russian treasure." It was Mohammed himself in a soft, faltering voice. "The mysterious cases—Kaitos ordered me to open them."

"What was inside?" Hasan asked gently.

Isa gestured to Mohammed to shut up, but he kept talking.

"One was like the inside of a radio. Electronic stuff. Also an explosive charge."

"How do you know?"

Mohammed vomited a small amount of blood and continued. "I was in the army. It looked like C-4. A shaped charge."

The boy gently wiped Mohammed's face.

"Was that all?" Hasan couldn't understand what had been so toxic.

"No, there was something else, god help me. In each case was a small half-sphere of a strange metal. It looked like white steel but was heavier than lead. I thought it might be platinum."

"You picked it up?"

"Yes. It felt hot, and it glowed."

"Glowed?" Hasan was incredulous.

"Glowed, then began to burn. Horrible pain. I dropped it."

Hasan looked grim. He suddenly understood what had happened.

"How long ago did this occur? When did you get sick?"

"Yesterday. I became sick within minutes. Vomit. Headache. Weakness. My skin began to swell . . ." He retched again.

Hasan gave him some morphine and antibiotics, and then, with Jack's help, swaddled his burned hands with wet compresses. Mohammed began to lose consciousness.

"That's all I can do for now." Hasan looked sharply at Isa. "Did anyone else touch what was inside those cases?"

Isa answered. "No, Kaitos only truly trusts his cousins. Mohammed was alone."

Amir was disturbed. "What is this curse?"

Hasan shook his head. "Something I'm afraid I can't cure." He then translated what Mohammed had said for Jack.

"Doctor, is it possible . . ." Jack hesitated for a moment as he recalled Tatra's terrible warnings to Julia. Her prophecy seemed to be coming true.

"Jack?"

He blurted out his darkest thought. "That this man has radiation poisoning?"

"Yes, these are the classic symptoms." Hasan's face darkened. "God help us, Jack, I think these foolish pirates have stolen some kind of atomic device."

47. DEADLY TREASURE

Jack and Hasan were brought back to Kaitos, who had established a throne of sorts in a large, half-roofed, concrete ruin, possibly the old British officers' quarters.

"I've treated the gunshot cases," Hasan reported. "One is ready to travel but the other can't be moved for a few days."

Kaitos nodded. "And the third man, my cousin?"

"He's dying from acute radiation poisoning. Do you know what that is?"

"I'm not sure." Kaitos looked uncomfortable.

"He's come into contact with the incredibly toxic metals used in nuclear reactors and atomic bombs."

Kaitos's jaw dropped. "Atomic?"

"May I inspect your mysterious treasure?"

Kaitos recovered his composure. "Of course, that's why you're here. Amir, take the doctor and the boy to the other bunker."

"No, Kaitos, not the boy. It's too dangerous. Just me. And Amir must wait outside."

"As you wish." Kaitos smiled.

Jack started to protest, but Hasan raised his index finger to his lips. "Shhh."

Dr. Hasan took a thermometer out of his kit, along with some paper and a pen. He disappeared with Amir.

Kaitos had Isa take Jack outside. He ordered another man to fetch them some food. Isa and Jack squatted on their haunches, eating the meal in silence.

Jack kept looking anxiously at his watch. Every additional second that Dr. Hasan stayed in the bunker increased his risk.

Hasan, looking haggard, returned fifteen minutes later. Amir took him straight into Kaitos's bunker, and a minute later he called out for Isa to bring Jack in as well.

"I've explained to Kaitos that we need a moment to analyze this data before giving an opinion." Hasan's forehead was covered with sweat but he was quite calm.

"Doctor, what did you find?" Jack was desperate.

"First, Jack, help me figure out what all this means. You know some Russian, don't you?"

"Sure, I can read a little. . . . It's the obligatory second language of aeronautical science."

Hasan spread out his notes. He had carefully transcribed Cyrillic writing from the two stolen cases.

Jack carefully scanned the notes. His hands were trembling.

"Doctor, I should never have let you go into that cave!"

"It had to be done, Jack. Tell Kaitos what the inscriptions say. I'll translate."

Jack shook his head and began. "There are lots of numbers and technical codes whose meaning I can't decipher, but the key phrases are: 'Unit One: Attila Device; 2 KT; Semipalatinsk 1987. Unit Two: Arming Module. Lethal Plutonium!'"

Kaitos was impatient. "What does all this mean?"

"I'll let Jack answer," said Hasan. "He's an engineer and also a peace activist. He knows more about this stuff than I do."

"Peace activist?" The meaning entirely escaped Kaitos.

Jack got straight to the point. "This is a Soviet-made nuclear device, a so-called 'suitcase' bomb. It was developed during the 1980s at the major Soviet nuclear test facility—Semipalatinsk—in Kazakhstan. It has the destructive power of two thousand tons of TNT."

As Hasan translated, Jack could see that Kaitos was still mostly in the dark.

"Look, Kaitos, this is a small atomic bomb. It is powerful enough to blow up this entire island. One attaché case is the bomb itself; it already contains half of the quantity of the incredibly dangerous metal, plutonium, needed to produce the explosion. The other half required for a chain reaction was nested in lead in the second case—it needs to be installed in the first case for the bomb to work, but this has be done in a special facility. If anyone attempts to handle the plutonium without adequate protection, they'll die. Plutonium is the most toxic substance in the universe."

Kaitos still didn't comprehend the technical details, but he got the big picture. He was now a one-man nuclear superpower.

"Ah, now I understand why the Russians fought to the death to protect their little treasure. This bomb must be worth more than a whole oil field."

Jack thought he could hear Kaitos licking his chops. Greed shone like searchlights from his eyes.

"No, you don't get the point," Hasan yelled. "The plutonium will kill all of you. You'll die horrible, agonizing deaths like Mohammed."

He turned away from Kaitos to address the rest of the pirates. "And even if you could avoid the sickness, the Americans will track you down and destroy you. This bomb is a death curse, an evil *jinn*."

Kaitos's followers wore fear and alarm on their faces.

The pirate chief was furious at Hasan. "You're scaring my men—maybe I should feed you to the sharks anyway."

Just then Isa noticed a trickle of blood coming from Dr. Hasan's nose.

"Look, Kaitos," he exclaimed, "now he has the curse as well!"

Indeed, Dr. Hasan suddenly felt nauseated and weak. He vomited blood several times. Jack helped him sit down.

"It will kill us all, Kaitos, believe me," Dr. Hasan said softly. "You need to leave this island immediately. Save yourself and your men."

The young boy from the medical bunker ran up to Amir and spoke in his ear.

"Kaitos," Amir announced, "Mohammed is dead. His body is covered with blisters."

The pirates started arguing and shouting with Kaitos, who in turn ordered Amir to lock Jack and Hasan in the medical bunker. Dr. Hasan was already so weak that he had to lean on Jack for support.

48. THE DEAD MAN

Amir took them back to the medical bunker. The young boy and the pirate with the shoulder wound had already left. Before Amir bolted the door, he said with sincerity, "May God protect you!"

Jack and Hasan were left alone with the abdominal wound patient and Mohammed's corpse. While the Muslim custom calls for burying the dead quickly, apparently the pirates were too frightened by the plutonium "curse" to touch poor Mohammed's body.

Jack walked over to the body. The dead man's eyes were staring into infinity, so Jack gently shut them. He then covered him with a blanket.

He fetched a blanket and some water for Hasan, who was too weak to stand. The doctor popped some aspirin and took his own temperature.

"Not much else we can do right now." Hasan smiled weakly.

"Doctor, tell me the truth. How bad are you?"

"Don't look so grim, Jack. I may get very sick, but I won't die. Unlike Mohammed, I didn't touch the plutonium, so it is unlikely I received a fatal dosage. Maybe cancer in twenty years, but I should survive for now."

"You do look awful."

"True, I haven't felt this bad since the last time the Mets lost to the Yankees. But don't mope around worrying about me. Remember our patient over there—be sure to change his dressing. You should also give him some more morphine. Do you know how to do it?"

Jack nodded.

"I'm going to conk out for a few hours, and you should do the same. Wake me if the pirates decide to feed us to the sharks." Hasan managed an ironic smile. It was just past midnight.

49. DOOMSDAY

Jack awoke with a start. Light was creeping under the bunker's old rusted door, and he berated himself for sleeping through the night. He had dreamt he heard planes landing, their engines whining to a huge crescendo.

He checked on the condition of the others: Mohammed was still dead; Dr. Hasan was breathing heavily, but asleep; the wounded pirate was lying with his eyes wide open, obviously in pain.

After calming him with a few gentle words, Jack gave him some water and another morphine shot, and his eyelids soon collapsed. Jack carefully dressed the wound, thankful now that Conor had convinced him two summers ago to take an advanced wilderness first-aid course.

Conor. Julia. He shuddered as he thought about the night they had spent in the cave.

He had to get help.

The first step was to pound on the door until one of the pirates responded. Jack hit the door as hard as he could with the side of his fist. To his surprise, it opened.

The sun blinded him, and it took half a minute for his eyes to focus clearly.

The pirates were gone—that explained his dream about airplane engines. Even more remarkably, they had left behind all of the looted gear, including Conor's kayak, as well as a considerable quantity of water and food. It was all stacked neatly outside the bunker door. Perhaps Kaitos was not such a bad character after all.

Jack immediately searched for his PC and booted up; it was still alive. The rest of the equipment looked undamaged as well.

He went back inside and gently woke Hasan. He gave the doctor some water and a couple of sweet dates. Hasan was feverish, so Jack took his temperature and gave him some more aspirin.

"Thanks, Dr. Davis." Hasan's smile cheered Jack.

"They're gone—all three boats. And Kaitos has left us all our gear and some food."

Hasan stopped smiling. He grasped Jack's forearm.

"Did you check the bomb bunker?"

"No, not yet."

Hasan was relieved. "Good; I was worried you might have exposed yourself."

"No. Remember, I know something about radiation safety. But we have to find out if they took the bomb or not."

"Of course, but you can't go inside. Mohammed dropped one of the plutonium half-spheres on the floor of the bunker. It was lying there when I entered last night."

Jack thought for a second. "What if I rig a rope to the door and pull it open from a distance? I can peer inside with our night-sight binoculars."

"OK, the exposure probably won't be hazardous. But don't hang around—take one look and get away fast."

"Roger. I'll be right back; you rest."

Jack quickly found the extra, unused climbing rope that Conor and Julia would probably give anything for right now, but it took him a few minutes to locate the remaining pair of binoculars equipped with infrared night vision.

The doomsday bunker was about fifteen hundred feet away. As he got near, he saw to his horror that the door was open and that one of the pirates was lying dead or unconscious about sixty feet from the entrance.

Jack dropped to one knee and peered through the binoculars. The pirate was lying in a pool of vomit and blood. His face—horribly swollen and raw—was almost unrecognizable, while his hands looked charred. Jack couldn't detect any chest movement or sign that the man was breathing.

He raised the binoculars and tried to look inside the bunker, but he was at too low an angle. He advanced another one hundred feet to the top of a small dune. Now he could see inside. The two briefcases were still there, although one had been moved. It was lying a few steps from the door and was partially open.

He turned on the infrared detector, which saw heat: suddenly the case near the door blazed like a neon light. Jack surmised that the poor pirate had picked up the plutonium and replaced it in its lead-lined case, getting only as far as the door before his radiation burns became excruciating. He must have dropped the case and staggered outside, where he now lay dead.

Although Hasan wouldn't approve, Jack had to find out for sure whether the man was dead, so he sprinted over.

The pirate was indeed dead, and Jack was horrified to discover that the grotesquely bloated face was that of Isa, Kaitos's cousin and the friendliest of their captors. Jack retreated in a run.

Hasan had propped himself up against the wall, but he still looked terrible.

"Were you careful? Is it still there?"

Jack explained what had happened.

"You did a brave thing. I don't think you'll have any symptoms, but when we get back we must thoroughly check you out. Now the important thing, Jack, is that the bomb is still here. If the pirates had taken it . . . my god . . . can you imagine where it might have ended up?"

"But they could still return for it, Doctor. What do we do? How are we going to help Conor and Julia?"

Jack's mind short-circuited in face of the triple urgencies of rescuing the kids in the cave, saving Dr. Hasan, and preventing an atomic bomb in a suitcase from ending up in the wrong hands.

"Maybe we should bury the bomb or throw it into the lagoon." Jack immediately realized that these were poor solutions, as well as suicidal.

Hasan coughed harshly. His throat was raw and his voice raspy. "Jack, I'm afraid you have been elected Atlas: the weight of the world is temporarily on your shoulders. Come up with a plan, son, and do it quickly. But don't let anyone know about the bomb." Hasan then collapsed.

50. JACK'S PLAN

Jack realized that there was no time for anxiety or self-pity. Hasan was right: his responsibilities were absurdly gigantic, but he had to act decisively and immediately.

He went back outside. As he stared at his pile of gear, a plan suddenly crystallized in his mind, like a genie coaxed out of a jar. After all, he did have his microbats and a kayak.

The first priority was to send a bat back to Camp Terbec with a message detailing the location of the cave and an urgent plea to rescue

Conor and Julia. It was fortunate that he had installed the homing beacon at Terbec.

Jack took out a notepad and scribbled a series of equations. He calculated that microwave power plus jet boosters should put Terbec within range, even if he and Dr. Hasan were marooned on the outermost of the uninhabited islands. He hunted in one of the packs and found his GPS. Good news: they were on one of The Brothers, the islands nearest to Socotra.

He quickly set up the microwave transmitter, and now he needed a bat: Morphy the Great was the obvious choice. He fitted him with the little engines he had used in the Mt. Wilson trial, fed them fuel with an eyedropper, placed a note about Conor and Julia in the bat's nose, then cranked up as much microwave energy as possible. He decided not to put anything in the note about his and Dr. Hasan's plight—nothing must tip the wrong parties off to the location of the bomb.

Jack gave Morphy a good-luck kiss on the nose and placed him on the low roof of the bunker. He sat on the sand and typed with frenzy into his laptop, causing Morphy to zoom aloft. The microwave beam would propel him to the edge of Socotra, the jets would boost him as far as Hadibo, and then the batteries would take him the rest of the way home in about twenty minutes. If all went well, aid would soon be on its way to Conor and Julia.

Now to save Hasan and the world.

Jack looked admiringly at Conor's prized kayak. His little brother, who had the agility and skill of a native Greenlander, wouldn't be daunted by the Indian Ocean in early February. However, Jack knew that his own ability was only mediocre. His entire sea-kayaking experience was confined to Dublin Bay and once off Santa Monica—not a strong résumé for the adventure he was about to attempt.

But Jack also knew he had no choice. At least he was a very strong long-distance swimmer, although that might not get him very far in the famously shark-infested waters of the Gulf of Aden.

Working as fast as possible, he loaded the kayak with some survival gear, including the GPS device, a diver's knife, and his Arabic dictionary. Intuition also advised him to take along his precious vial of E-dust and the small receiver that went with it. He wiggled into Conor's wetsuit and put his hiking shoes back on in case he had to negotiate razor-sharp coral.

A grim task remained. After locating an entrenching tool amongst the pirate's supplies, he dragged poor Mohammed's body out of the bunker and buried him under a few feet of sand, leaving the small shovel upright as a temporary gravemarker. He felt guilty for not burying Isa as well, but he was running out of time.

Inside the bunker, Hasan was awake. His condition remained poor but stable. Jack brought in lots of water, food, and some extra blankets. He told the doctor about Morphy.

"Brilliant move! But you didn't disclose our location, did you?"

Jack shook his head.

"Good, there is always a chance of the information falling into the wrong hands. We can't let the Americans or even the Yemeni government find out where the bomb is. Some sinister game is afoot. Best to go directly to the United Nations, or even better, to the world press. Can you find a way to do that?"

"I'll try, Doctor; I'll find a radio or cell phone somehow. But how about you? I have a lot on my plate—it might take me a week to get back to you."

"I'll survive. The pirates have left enough food and water for a month."

"How about him?" Jack pointed to the wounded pirate.

"He's quickly getting better. In another day he'll be able to take care of me."

"Well then, I am off on a wee boat trip." Jack was glad that Hasan had no idea how dangerous a journey he was embarking on.

Hasan squeezed his hand. "Top of the ninth, bases are loaded, and we need your run to win the game. Think Babe Ruth."

"Thanks, Coach." Jack laughed and went outside. It was actually a gorgeous day: the weather was clear, and the notorious local winds were temporarily on vacation.

So, Jack had one stroke of luck. Unfortunately, the survival of the expedition now depended on his having an entire hand of lucky cards. Morphy needed to reach Terbec, Conor and Julia had to ward off dragons, and he had to avoid becoming a shark's dinner. Jack pushed the kayak into the lagoon and started paddling toward the distant gray coast of Socotra.

CHAPTER NINE: *The Labyrinth*

*Minos arranged to sacrifice young men and women
to the flesh-eating Minotaur by shutting them into the
Labyrinth, where they would wander, hopelessly lost,
until the Minotaur caught and devoured them.*
GREEK MYTHOLOGY

*I*nside the mouth of the cave, the wind was whipping up the bat guano into toxic white dust. Julia was nauseated. She also knew that bat droppings sometimes contain spores of a fungus that can cause the deadly respiratory infection known as histoplasmosis. She put on her climbing helmet and diving goggles and tied her handkerchief around her mouth. Weasel was hiding in his pouch.

"Let's get out of here," she mumbled to Conor, who was similarly attired.

They carried their heavy waterproof duffel bags over a series of guano mounds and through an obstacle course of fallen limestone boulders. One hundred fifty feet inside, the wind subsided and the cave rapidly became pitch-black.

"I guess we're salamander bait from here on," Conor complained, as he turned on his carbide miner's light.

"Speak for yourself, mortal," Julia the Witch kidded.

In truth, neither of them was too worried about Tatra's dragons at the moment. Their overriding concern was to get deep enough into the cave to avoid tangling with the evening's outrush of hungry bats. Soon, tens of thousands of the little mousetails would rouse from their slumber and depart en masse from the mouth of the cave. It would be messy to be in their way.

Julia shone her laser flashlight on the ceiling ahead. They were in a large hall plastered with bat guano, but only a few groups of upside-down mousetails were visible in the farthest eaves and cracks. A solitary bat fluttered by: it had a ratlike tail as long as its furry little body. The main colony was still ahead.

"What do you know about these bats?" Conor asked. "They look like flying mice."

Julia lowered her handkerchief. "*Rhinopomatidae* are probably the most primitive insectivorous bats, but they have no fossil record so we don't know when they evolved. This particular species also doesn't seem to hibernate during the winter. Not much known because it has hardly been studied.

On the other hand, their cousins, the *Rhinopoma microphyllum*, are famous."

"Famous for what?"

"They inhabit the Egyptian pyramids. Sometimes when archaeologists open ancient tombs, the little *microphyllums* fly out. No one knows how they get so far inside the pyramids or what they eat. Legend blames them for the deaths of many Egyptologists."

"You mean like in the *Curse of the Mummy's Tomb*?"

"Yes, but it may be more than just superstition. It's possible that some people have actually died from histoplasmosis contracted from their guano. That's why we need to keep our faces covered."

"Thanks for sharing that bit of reassuring information." Conor frowned and pulled his bandanna back over his mouth. Julia chuckled.

Soon they came to a series of deep, apparently bottomless cracks in the floor. But they were only a few feet wide, and Julia and Conor needed just a moderate stride to vault across them.

They left the entry hall of the cave and entered a smaller chamber. Conor abruptly stopped and pointed his flashlight on the ceiling. He illuminated a huge chute that appeared to be blocked by a boulder about fifty feet higher up. He carefully studied it for a moment, then dismissed it as a possible escape route.

A shape swished by Julia, then another, and then another. Bats were beginning to rush at them, and they could hear high-pitched pandemonium just ahead. Weasel's head popped up out of his pouch.

Conor led them into the cathedral-sized hall that was the principal home of Socotra's mousetails. His powerful flashlight beam sent a tremor through the population. Thousands of little yellow eyes winked back from their upside-down roosts.

"My god." Conor was flabbergasted at the size of the colony. "This is bat city."

A rain of bat guano and urine fell from the ceiling, and the stench of ammonia was almost overpowering.

Every step the kids took seemed to excite dozens of bats and cause the animals to drop from the ceiling and dive close to their heads. Soon the path in front of them was a nervous thicket of wildly zigzagging flying mice. The noise, like the smell of the chamber, was excruciating: it was a cacophonous composite of berserk cackling and chalk being screeched across a blackboard.

Julia, who ordinarily loved bats, found the chaos disturbing. It brought back the frightening memory of the strange frenzy amongst the crabs before they attacked her. She kept reminding herself that bats' extraordinary echolocation ability would prevent them from colliding with one another or entangling themselves in her hair, but she couldn't help wincing as the little animals fluttered within inches of her face.

Suddenly the screeching subsided for a moment, then rose to a crescendo. The bat colony was detaching itself from the ceiling and dissolving into flight.

Conor and Julia instinctively threw themselves to the ground and covered their heads, while Weasel jumped out of his pouch and ran behind a rock. The walls of the huge chamber vibrated from the sudden flapping of almost 50,000 pairs of tiny wings. There was a rush of air like the exhaust of a jet engine.

Perhaps ten minutes passed as they lay on the floor of the cave. Finally, when the cave was almost quiet, Conor got up, dusted off a heavy layer of bat guano, and aimed his flashlight at the ceiling. The colony was gone.

He gently helped Julia to her feet. She was shaken and embarrassed.

52. THE DRAGONS' DINNER TABLE

"I'm really turning into a wimp, aren't I," she said bitterly.

Conor just shook his head. "Ease up on yourself. This last week has been a horror movie: centipedes, crabs, witches, pirates, and bats." He affectionately squeezed her arm. "Let's go look for dragons."

Julia gathered Weasel from his hiding place. He growled as a lone mousetail flew by.

After about one hundred feet, they came to a huge flat slab of limestone that looked like a giant altar. Perhaps it was.

"Julia, what in the McMurphy is that?" Conor's miner's light illuminated the cave floor in front of the "altar": it was strewn with bones.

Julia bent over and picked up a skull.

"A goat." She unhooked a powerful flashlight from her climbing harness and scrutinized the floor around them. It was littered with the violently dismembered remains of sacrificial goats.

Weasel, who was sniffing around the bones, smelled something that was greatly agitating him. He stayed close to Julia.

Conor boosted himself to the top of the limestone slab and began to examine the network of incised lines on its surface. "Julia, quick, come look at this!"

Carved into the stone were bizarre symbols and words formed from several different languages. Julia recognized only the Greek word *mene:* "moon."

"Oh my god!" In the very center of the enormous rock Conor had found a life-size outline of a creature about eight feet long. It closely resembled one of the giant salamanders in Julia's slides.

"*Andrias davidianus,*" Julia mumbled. "Or, rather an extremely close homologue, perhaps the result of parallel evolution. Incredible."

Suddenly the scientist in Julia kicked in. "Conor, we must carefully document this site. Let's unpack the photography equipment."

"Yeah, I would feel a wee bit safer if we set up the strobes." Conor stared apprehensively into the darkness ahead of them. Julia was too absorbed in the excitement of discovery to remember that they were presently standing in the middle of the dragons' dinner table.

53. FRUSTRATION AND INFATUATION

"So what have the dragons eaten since Tatra was last here?" Conor asked nervously.

Julia chuckled. "Don't worry. The sacrificial goats could only have been a gourmet treat, not their regular cuisine. But I'm baffled by their food source. Something this big needs a reliable supply of fish, birds, or small mammals."

Julia set up their photo equipment. She wanted to take a panoramic shot using their strobe lights to illuminate the whole altar end of the cave chamber.

"Better put on your shades, Conor," she warned.

Conor obliged, and Julia protectively cradled Weasel in her arms.

Then she lit up the cave. Baby bats cackled angrily in the ceiling.

The vast room was perhaps three hundred by two hundred by eighty feet in volume. Ahead of Julia and Conor it narrowed once again into a tunnel about fifteen feet high. Above the mouth of that tunnel, however, was a second, narrower opening. It slanted upward toward the surface at a steep angle.

"Julia, would you be OK for a few minutes while I climbed up and explored that chute?"

"Sure, but be careful."

Conor spidered his way to the upper hole, using the plentiful handholds in the rough limestone. As he boosted himself into the opening, he was blasted by moist air.

"Julia, there's wind," he shouted down. "This opens to the surface."

Perhaps it would be easy to escape the cave after all.

Conor crawled through a chokepoint where part of the roof had collapsed and emerged inside a steeply tilted tunnel. The surface was moist and covered with guano and algae: very slippery going indeed. Several times Conor slipped and slid backwards to his starting point.

On the fourth try he reached the upper end. It was another of what cavers call "breakdowns": in this case, a combination of a partially collapsed roof and debris fallen from higher up. Conor searched for an opening big enough to squeeze through. Seeing none, he scooped away dirt and gravel with his hands until he had enlarged one of the small holes. Then, with his body relaxed and fully extended, he slithered like a snake through the narrow space.

Again he was in an open tunnel, larger than the last but equally steep, wet, and slippery. Fortunately there was a crack along the wall which gave him a handhold. He climbed upward about sixty feet. Directly overhead but agonizingly out of reach was a chimney, which was blocked by a large, rounded boulder. There were plenty of small holes, but none bigger than a fist. The wind howled and water drizzled down the walls; it must be raining up on the plateau.

Conor calculated that he was now only thirty feet from the surface. He tried to climb up the wide chimney, but the side walls were too smooth and slippery—zero coefficient of friction.

He figured he might be able to return with his hammer and enough bolts to rig some holds to the top, but it looked hardly worth the effort: the boulder lodged in the mouth of the chimney was too large to move. It would be like trying to escape from a wine bottle by pushing out the cork from below.

Salvation was so close and yet so far.

Meanwhile, as Julia carefully photographed the inscriptions on the altar stone, in her mind she was trying to calculate the danger of continuing to explore the cave—now that they had proof of the salamanders' existence—versus Conor's suicidal plan to scale the overhang without a rope or belay. It still seemed more sensible to push ahead. Animals that ate goats didn't necessarily eat humans . . .

Suddenly Julia had the sensation that she was being watched. Weasel growled. She turned around abruptly, expecting the worst, but there was nothing there. She stood up and focused the powerful strobe light toward the dark end of the tunnel ahead. Something moved. Or did it?

She was still pondering whether she had actually seen something when Conor literally dropped down from the hole in the ceiling. She decided to conceal her anxiety. Perhaps he had good news.

"Find the way home?" she asked expectantly.

"Frustration tunnel, I'm afraid. We're bottled in by a huge boulder at the very top, just a few feet from the surface."

"Could we move it a little, or dig around it?"

"Too heavy to shift, and if we tried to excavate the wall, the boulder would probably end up in our laps. We're snookered."

"What now?"

"Well, I promised you twenty-four hours, so it's up to you." Conor nervously eyed the dark tunnel ahead. "Do you still want to forge ahead?"

A few straggler bats fluttered by. Julia didn't answer.

"Julia, are you OK?"

"No, I have a confession. I may have seen something ahead in the cave."

"What do you mean by 'may have'?"

"Conor, I just don't know. Perhaps it's the pitiful spooked-out state I've been in since Ras Momi, or maybe I really saw something move in the shadows . . . Weasel was agitated . . . I can't be sure."

"Well, don't beat yourself up any more." Conor patted her on the shoulder. "Let's keep going a little further. We know these things are sensitive to light, so we'll hope our headlamps scare them away; as a backup we have the strobe lights and our climbing hammers."

Again, Julia failed to respond.

"Julia?"

She unexpectedly came into Conor's arms, and they hugged for a long minute. "I don't want you eaten by a salamander," she whispered fiercely in his ear. "Let's stay close together." She kissed him on the cheek.

Conor was too overwhelmed to speak. He could only nod and hope Julia didn't see the tears welling up in his eyes.

Julia had always been his and Jack's idol, their very bravest and most beautiful friend, the most dashing girl either had ever met. But as the younger brother, Conor had always imagined in the back of his mind that Jack and Julia would someday run off to start their own anarchist science colony on an ice floe or volcano.

If it was a surprise to him when Jack talked about the mysterious Lucy Chen in California, it was a thousand times more surprising when Julia sought an embrace—perhaps some other design was working itself out. He shivered as he looked at Julia. She was gorgeous, even covered with bat guano.

Julia playfully pushed him away. "A little squeeze make you speechless, Mr. Blarney Stone? Your Irish wit go AWOL?"

Conor blushed, then laughed and shook his head. "Well, it'll be a first date to remember: the dragon dinner party. After you, my dear." He pointed ahead toward the darkness.

54. LITTLE FISH

After about fifty feet the tunnel began to curve to the right. Although the walls grew further apart, the ceiling was now low enough to occasionally scrape the tops of their climbing helmets. The heavy duffel bags were taking a toll.

"I think we probably need to set up camp," suggested Conor, his muscles aching from nearly eighteen hours of climbing and hauling. "I'm totally knackered."

"Me too," sighed Julia. "Let's just see what's around that column ahead."

An ornate column of calcite, built up by centuries of slow mineralized dripping, blocked the way ahead.

"Quite beautiful. Looks like one of the entry columns in the Parthenon," observed Julia.

"Or the Temple of Death," quipped Conor, as they squeezed by.

The tunnel abruptly opened into yet another large chamber. Under their helmet lights the floor shimmered like quicksilver.

"A sump," said Julia, using the caver's term for an underground body of water.

Conor shone his light at the edge, where the stone was opalescent, and then across the water, which completely covered the floor of the hall.

"Julia, use your flashlight. See how deep it is."

She knelt at the edge of the mysterious water and shone her light into the depths. The pearly bottom reflected the light back.

"Maybe fifteen feet deep in the center, but it looks like the left side is only knee high; I can't see all the way to the end. Shall we chance it?"

"Your call."

"OK, I'll lead." Julia felt her old confidence coming back.

The water was achingly cold and closer to hip high in places. On the other hand, it was deep enough to float the heavy waterproof duffels.

Weasel was a great swimmer, so Julia let him cross by himself—and he immediately went berserk. And so did Conor.

"Leaping lizards!" Conor swore and jumped up on a little ledge.

Julia was petrified but stayed where she was. Then, as something seemed to nibble at her ankle, she started to shriek but suddenly began to laugh.

Weasel had a fish between his teeth.

"Conor, look—cave fish." The sump was full of blind minnow-like fish about four inches long.

Ahead was a small beach, and above it, a dry area leading to a large tunnel that plunged downward at a steep angle into the depths. Julia and Conor pulled their duffel bags out of the water while the famished Weasel dined on the fish.

They chose a cozy spot behind some boulders for their camp. Conor gathered rocks to complete a defensive wall; Julia first set up the strobe light, then organized the bivouac. A half hour later, they were huddled in their little fortress.

Weasel was sprawled at the foot of Julia's sleeping bag, hiccuping from his fish dinner. Julia had used her sleeping bag and changed into some long underwear, while Conor, his teeth chattering, tried to wring out their soggy clothes.

"Well, at least we've solved the puzzle of the dragons' diet," he said between chatters.

"If only to replace it with the mystery of what the fish eat. Did you see how many fish there were? A stupendous population for a cave ecosystem." Julia glanced at Weasel's bulging tummy.

"I managed to catch a couple." Conor handed Julia a Ziploc bag containing the fish specimens. "Wish I knew something about fish," he said apologetically.

"They look like riceditch killifish," replied Julia.

"Come again?"

"A fish with tiny eyes found in the American South. They have blind cave cousins; I read about them in one of my speleobiology books. But these are certainly a new species, if not a new family or genus."

"So you're the discoverer. What do you want to name them?"

Julia gulped. This was actually rather monumental: the discovery of a new species. She thought for a long moment.

"Let's name them after Tatra. We'll call them *Tatrasidae*. OK?"

"I hope she appreciates the honor."

"Get in your bag: you must be freezing."

Conor crawled into his bag next to Julia's. They felt relatively secure: they were well fortified and had Weasel as their Socotran equivalent of a guard dog.

55. THE SKULL

Weasel snarled, and Julia awoke with a start. She pushed the button that controlled the powerful strobe lights, and the cave briefly exploded in illumination. Peering through a space between the boulders she saw something disappearing into the downward-plunging tunnel.

Conor erupted from his sleeping bag and grabbed his climbing hammer.

"It's OK. It's gone," Julia said soberly. She looked at her watch. "My god, we've been asleep for nearly seven hours." She tried to calm Weasel, who was shaking all over.

"Close call?"

"I don't know," replied Julia. "We still don't know if they are truly aggressive toward humans—perhaps just curious. And our strobe lights certainly deter them."

Conor rubbed his eyes and yawned. "Let's make breakfast."

They broke out some freeze-dried rations and boiled some water for tea on their Primus stove while they discussed what to do. Conor proposed that they continue their exploration for four more hours. If they failed to find a way out, they would return to his Plan B. Julia reluctantly agreed.

"Should we leave some of this gear here? I'm tired of being a sherpa," Conor complained.

"OK, let's leave the camp as is, including most of our food supply and the photo equipment. But I think we should still take the scuba gear. We might have to swim a flooded passage."

Conor frowned: the scuba gear was the heaviest equipment they carried, and he was not particularly keen about going underwater. But Julia had more caving experience, so he accepted her wisdom.

"OK, Great Leader, whatever you say. But what is our defense if we run into the dragons?"

"I'm going to let Weasel go ahead as our scout; I have my powerful flashlight, and you take the flash unit from one of the cameras. Hopefully that will be enough light to affect their photosensitive skin. Otherwise, we run." Julia smiled.

Conor just shook his head.

It became immediately obvious that travel was going to be much more hazardous than it was yesterday. The next pitch descended down a breathtakingly steep series of ledges and short falls. Fortunately there was plenty of traction and innumerable handholds.

"Welcome to the 'Devil's Staircase,'" said Conor, as he helped Julia lower her duffel bag through a well-like passage. He offered her some climbing chalk. "Hard to believe your favorite monsters can actually negotiate this."

Julia nodded. Indeed, she couldn't imagine a basically aquatic animal the size of *Andrias* climbing up this chute.

As they plunged deeper, their carbide headlamps illuminated an underground world of fantastic baroque beauty. The walls were blistered with delicate egg-shell calcite, and every cavity was full of jewel-like crystals or deposits of cave coral. They worked their way carefully around fragile stalactites and hanging curtains of pastel travertine.

"Do you hear something?" Conor asked nervously. Julia stopped and listened.

"A distant roar," she answered. "A waterfall?"

As they came to the bottom of the long chute, the tunnel narrowed and again became horizontal. The walls here were stark limestone, with little of the speleolithic structures they had just seen. It looked like it was flooded part of the year, and there were occasional pools of murky water.

Meanwhile, the noise was becoming deafening. Weasel returned in a great state of excitement.

"Waterfall scare you?" Conor asked him playfully. Weasel glared.

"No, I think he's found something. We'd better be careful."

They laid the duffels down and prepared themselves to confront an unknown menace. Julia turned on her flashlight while Conor wielded his flashbulb and rock hammer.

"We look ridiculous," he complained. "Like some bumbling vampire hunters about to walk into Dracula's crypt."

Julia fingered the moon charm that Tatra had given her. For safety's sake, she decided to put Weasel back into his pouch.

The three explorers nervously moved forward. Their lights began to illuminate a chaotic spectacle of falling and swirling water ahead of them.

As Julia shone her light on the floor ahead, Weasel hissed through his teeth. White bones lay scattered about.

"Oh Weasel, you big coward," she scolded. "It's nothing but another dead goat."

"I wouldn't be so sure," said Conor in a tremulous voice. He had gone ahead to inspect the bones. "Look at this."

He held up a skull. It was human.

CHAPTER TEN: *The Shark Hunters*

*The Tiger Shark's jaws are so powerful they can bite through
the shells of large turtles. As well as turtles, other sharks, scavenged
livestock, and humans, Tiger Sharks also dine out on such attractive
delicacies as sea snakes, venomous jellyfish, and stingrays.*
AL SHINDAGAH MAGAZINE (1999)

A particular Socotran delicacy is shark liver.
VITALY NAUMKIN (1993)[22]

*M*orphy, Jack's reliable microbat, was now locked onto the homing beacon from Terbec. Like the real mousetails, he was rudely buffeted by offshore winds and roughly handled by the mountain thermals, but indefatigably he made his way home.

He landed next to the radio beacon Jack had erected in front of Samira's clinic. One of the local kids saw him approaching and set off the alarm, and the whole village dropped its work to watch Morphy land. Some of the kids applauded.

The locals, however, were not allowed to get near Morphy. A squad of tough-looking Yemeni Special Forces troops had occupied Terbec the night before. Samira, baby Omar, Anwar, and Hadad had all been taken into custody and moved down the mountain to the military camp in Hadibo. No one knew where Tariq was—presumably he was hiding in the mountains.

A large hand gently picked up Morphy and turned him over. The message from Jack was extracted and carefully read, then stuffed into a khaki pocket.

The tall Texan chuckled to himself. "Damn if these little pissants haven't gone and got themselves into a whole bucket of trouble." He took the cigar stub out of his mouth and ground it into the dirt with a heavy combat boot.

Some of the villagers were imploring him for information about the fate of Samira and the others. He coldly ignored them. Let the intelligence boys, if they could, sort out the innocent from the guilty. His job—which he fiercely loved—was tracking, hunting, and, occasionally, killing. Location and pretext weren't particularly important.

Colonel Strong returned to his Hummer and radioed the rest of his Delta Force team at the airport.

"You boys think you can get your Black Hawk up here pronto? No, that's too long," he barked. "I want your butts in the air now. Pick me up in Terbec. Two of our targets are stuck in a cave. Yeah, that's right. We're gonna do some more huntin'."

Jack now regretted all the times he had been too busy with home-work to go kayaking with Conor around Howth Peninsula or in Dublin Bay. His brother was a protégé of his Inuit friend Qav, who in turn had been trained by the world sea-kayaking idol and Greenlandic national champion Maligiaq.

Conor loved punching his way through a heavy chop or sculling in a confused sea. He was schooled in all the esoteric techniques of the "Eskimo roll," self-rescue, and survival in a bad ocean. Jack, on the other hand, just knew the raw basics of the Greenlandic style. He was a Sunday afternoon kayaker, not a competitive athlete like his brother.

Yet here he was in a wild sea with the fate of the world on his shoul-ders. "Fool," he whispered to himself, as a heavy swell almost turned him over. The biggest danger was being turned sideways by the first wave, then clobbered broadside by the second. He wasn't sure how to handle a wet exit from a capsized kayak in these waters.

Ordinarily he would at least wear a life vest, but the pirates forgot to leave one behind. Instead he was outfitted in Conor's undersized *tuiliq*, the sealskin kayaking garment that has been used in the Arctic for mil-lennia. It did an admirable job of keeping him warm and dry, but its buoyancy underwater was another question.

It was late afternoon and the day was still gorgeous, despite the wind pushing heavy swells toward Africa. Jack kept trying to focus on his technique—keeping his blade canted at the right angle and remem-bering to use torso rotation rather just his arms in the power stroke—but his mind kept straying to the colorful topic of marine fauna in the western Indian Ocean.

Like it or not, the Gulf of Aden was home to a fabulous diversity of dangerous shark and ray species. Indeed, sharks were the livelihood of Socotran and Yemeni fishermen, who dried and salted the meat for sale in Arabia and exported the more valuable fins and livers to China.

Already today Jack had seen innumerable rays and smaller sharks, as well as one very high and sharply pointed dorsal fin, probably belong-ing to a big hammerhead. It swam by nonchalantly at a distance, although hammerheads in less happy moods had been known to take huge bites out of surfboards, small boats, and swimmers' legs. He hoped the great carnivores would think his kayak was a fellow shark and not a tasty whale or porpoise.

His arms ached. Although Conor had repeatedly showed him how to use his back and abdominal muscles to relieve the strain on his arms, something in his technique was wrong; at this rate, he would soon cramp up. Socotra, meanwhile, seemed like a receding mirage. Landfall looked no closer than it had four hours earlier when he had started out.

Jack was meditating on his grim prospects when he was suddenly hit by what he at first thought was a torpedo—something clobbered the right side of the kayak and almost toppled it over. He used desperate sculling brace strokes to stabilize himself. The skin of the kayak was badly bruised but not quite punctured.

He looked around in panic but saw nothing. Torpedo, rock, sea turtle . . . his mind reeled off the possibilities. Perhaps a big manta ray? Just then he saw something that froze the blood in his veins.

The dorsal fin was smaller and more toothlike than the hammerhead's, but the body underneath the water was larger. In fact, it was huge, at least thirteen feet long. As it sped toward him he could see the short blunt snout and the whitish underbelly, as well as the vertical gray stripes on its back and along its sides. The body tapered sleekly to a long, slender caudal fin.

It was a tiger shark. Great whites and hammerheads kill humans because they mistake them for marine mammals, but only the tiger shark is a true man-eater. This was not a case of mistaken identity: it was trying to devour Jack.

He had only a few terrifying seconds to take some deep breaths before the second broadside blow completely capsized the kayak.

He was upside down in the water. Panic now would kill him for sure. For a split second he considered his options, then he pushed himself out of his seat and twisted his body around. He reached both hands up one side of the kayak, grasped the chine, and then hoisted himself up. His head and shoulders were out of the water, and he could breathe.

He waited for the bite, but the great shark seemed in no hurry to eat him. It circled around the kayak once, then swam in a wide arc before resuming its initial attack position; it clearly intended to hit him at high speed. Jack imagined either being bitten in half or carried off whole into the deep.

He struggled to climb on the back of the kayak or to right it, but he had no luck, and besides, the kayak's side was punctured. The *tuiliq* was too encumbering to allow him to swim free, so he desperately dog-paddled, pushing the kayak ahead of him.

The tiger shark seemed to find this amusing; it let Jack paddle for a few minutes until he was totally exhausted. Then it came: its speed and grace were extraordinary. There was no time for final thoughts, just flashing images of his Mom, Conor, and Julia. He closed his eyes and waited to die.

There was chaos and noise, but no pain. He opened his eyes. He was in a pool of reeking blood. "Oh my god," he thought. "The shark has bitten me in half." He wanted to scream, but he felt a cramp in his leg. Did he still have a leg?

Jack looked around. About twenty feet away the shark was floating upside down, bleeding massively from wounds in the head and heart area. The blood wasn't Jack's.

58. LUCKY MAN

A fisherman dove into the red swell—he wanted to put a grappling hook into the shark before it sank. A big tiger like this one was worth a small fortune, perhaps the larger part of a dowry.

On the prow of the sleek little outboard-powered *hawri*, another smiling fisherman was holding a smoking rifle. Jack would learn later that the man, whose name was Yahya, had skillfully shot the shark dead.

He and his two brothers had been tracking the giant tiger shark for two days, and they were delighted that Jack had inadvertently volunteered to play the role of bait. At the same time, they were flabbergasted to find a young *nasrani* defying the sea gods in a strange little craft even narrower than their *hawri*.

They pulled Jack into the boat and rescued his waterproof pack. Conor's kayak was tied up to the *hawri*'s slender stern.

Jack was still in shock at being alive. Yahya slapped him on the back.

"Lucky man, lucky man." He was about Jack's age and wore a huge grin.

"*Titkallam inglizi?*" Jack gasped. "You speak English?"

"Little English, yes. But you, lucky man. Shark very terrible. Eat one cousin, yes." Yahya counted on his fingers trying to remember the correct English word. "Four year ago. Eat cousin. Very bad fish."

Yahya urged Jack to relax and handed him a jug of fresh water. For the next half hour, the three young fishermen battled to keep the dead shark afloat. One of them ran a small tattered red flag up their little mast.

Soon several other boats arrived. "My cousins," smiled Yahya. An older, white-bearded man took charge of the operation. After another half hour of hoisting, pulling, grunting, and sweating, the shark had been successfully winched aboard the largest boat, a diesel-powered *sambuq*.

Jack was also transferred aboard, along with his gear and kayak. "Please meet Thani, my uncle. He is great *nakhudhah* (captain)." Yahya then told the story of Jack and the shark.

Thani and his crew laughed uproariously. Again, everyone patted Jack on the back and shouted "lucky man"—apparently the two universally known words of English in the Gulf of Aden.

Jack asked Yahya if they were from Socotra.

Yahya shook his head and laughed. "No, Socotra men pirates. Our home Al-Mukallah." He pointed north toward the distant Hadramawt coast in eastern Yemen.

Jack suddenly remembered Muhammad, the friend that he and Conor had made in San'a.

"Do you know the family of Muhammad Qa'id al-Husayni?"

Yahya looked amazed. Instead of answering Jack, he went to get his uncle.

Thani stroked his beard and looked intently at Jack. He talked to Yahya for a minute or two.

"My uncle say, 'Why young *nasrani* in middle of sea'?"

Jack tried to explain that he had been kidnapped by pirates, that his brother and young friend were in great trouble, and that their leader, Dr. Hasan, was back on The Brothers, perhaps mortally ill.

Yahya didn't understand most of the story, but he was impressed by Jack's passion as well as his courage in attempting to paddle to Socotra in such dangerous waters. He again conversed with Thani, and they seemed to reach some kind of consensus.

"The al-Husaynis are friends. Same clan. They are close by. Yahya pointed toward Socotra on the horizon. "You lucky man again. They have radio, we have radio. Few fishermen have radio."

Thani went into his tiny cabin. A few minutes later he emerged. He smiled at Jack and began to speak. Yahya translated: "Al-Husayni know you. They come soon. They will rescue your friends."

59. THE ROC

The al-Husaynis had the only European-type diesel fishing boat operating in the waters near Socotra, and so they were the local equivalent of the Automobile Association for the entire al-Mukallah fishing community. Their big boat provisioned the fleet, rescued *sambuqs* and *hawris* in distress, stored catches, relayed emergency messages via radio, and if need be, defended the smaller vessels against pirate attacks.

Muhammed's brothers, Ibrahim and Jalal, spoke passable English and had spent long years working as oil-riggers in Bahrain, building up their savings to purchase the *Roc*, named after the giant Socotran bird of the Sinbad legends.

Two hours after his initial rescue, Jack was aboard the *Roc*, telling the al-Husaynis his fantastic story—although not, of course, the part about the stolen atomic bomb. They were astounded that Kaitos had let him live.

In turn, they told him about the extraordinary news of the last two days: the Greek freighter destroyed nearby (some said by an American missile), the U.S. fleet swarming all over the Gulf of Aden, and the recent arrests on Socotra. They asked Jack how they could help him.

"First," he explained, "I need to radio Terbec to tell them about my brother and our friend. Secondly, I need to return to The Brothers to rescue Dr. Hasan. Can you help me?"

"Of course," smiled Ibrahim, "a friend of our brother is practically our family. We'll do whatever we can to assist you."

Jack nodded. Once again he was amazed by Arab generosity toward strangers.

It was difficult to raise Terbec on the radio. Finally, Anwar answered. "Jack, is that really you?" He sounded uncharacteristically suspicious.

"Yes, Anwar, it's really me. I've been rescued by some kind fishermen."

"Where is Dr. Hasan? Your brother? Julia?"

Jack quickly told Anwar the gist of the story except for the plutonium. "Please, Anwar, Conor and Julia are in great danger; you must organize a rescue."

"Don't worry, Jack, your little flying machine arrived earlier today. The Americans are already looking for them."

"The Americans?"

"Yes, and I'm sure they're listening to us right now. I was just released from custody, but Samira, baby Omar, and Hadad are still being held in Hadibo. You're all on the 'Most Wanted' list."

Jack was uncomprehending. "But why, Anwar? What have we done?"

"I don't really know, but they seem to believe that you know the location of something of extraordinary value. All kinds of fantastic rumors are floating around—some fishermen even claim that the Americans sank a Greek freighter."

Jack, of course, could now fit some of the pieces together, although he was staggered by the idea of the U.S. Navy sinking the freighter raided by Kaitos. It sounded too far-fetched.

"Jack, are you still there?"

"Oh yes . . . sorry, Anwar."

"You better get off now. Rescue Hasan and try to make contact with the UN. I'll do everything I can here, but I think the Americans will rearrest me. In fact, I think I was released in the hope that we would contact each other."

"Be careful," Jack urged the all-too-wise former diplomat.

"Don't worry about me, my boy. Look after yourself and Hasan. God be with you. *Ma'a s-salama.*"

60. RESCUING HASAN

The al-Husayni brothers, ignoring the risks, hurried toward The Brothers at top speed. They retraced Jack's laborious four-hour kayak journey in about twenty-five minutes.

Roc entered the lagoon and tied up at the ruined concrete pier. Jack warned them to keep the engines running in case they needed to make a quick escape; they seemed more worried about the threat of Kaitos's return than the appearance of the American fleet.

Jack raced toward the medical bunker. He threw the door open, expecting the worst, but instead he found Hasan and the wounded pirate sitting up, sharing a cup of tea. They seemed equally astonished to see Jack.

"Jack, you're safe! I was so worried; I knew the sea would be too dangerous. Thank god you turned back."

"No, Dr. Hasan, I didn't turn back—I found help. There are friends outside with a boat. They'll take us back to Socotra. But what about him? Should he come with us?"

Hasan turned to look at his pirate patient. "This is Amir's cousin, Nasr. He is very grateful that we saved his life."

The handsome young Somali pirate with the bandage wrapped around his middle smiled shyly at Jack.

"We've had a long talk—he understands the immense danger of the atomic device. He'll stay here and warn away anyone who attempts to land. But I have promised we'll return for him within a week." Hasan repeated himself in Arabic, and Nasr nodded.

"Will he be all right?"

"Absolutely. I've instructed him to take antibiotic tablets and showed him how to change his own dressings, and there is still plenty of food and water. He's actually quite a good kid. I trust him."

"We need to hurry then."

Jack helped Hasan to his feet, and both bowed *"Salaams"* to Nasr. Hasan reminded him not to get near the atomic bunker.

Hasan was a little dizzy, but he soon found his balance and was able to walk to the *Roc*. Jack was much encouraged by his strong recovery, although he was still alarmed by the evil-looking rashes on his hands and forearms.

Hasan saw the concern in Jack's eyes. "Don't worry, kid, I'll be fine. Any word about Julia and your brother?"

"There's a rescue expedition."

"Oh, that's great," said Hasan as he climbed down into the deck of the *Roc*. "Samira's taken charge, eh?"

"Not exactly," replied Jack.

61. LONG-DISTANCE CALL

The al-Husaynis, Jack's selfless friends, suggested a bold plan: they would head the *Roc* straight into the harbor at Qaysoh, Socotra's main fishing port, Jack and Hasan hidden in the fish storage compartment in case the military came aboard.

In fact, the *Roc* was stopped five miles off of Qaysoh by U.S. Navy Seals in a fast assault boat; a helicopter hovered high overhead. They were searching the entire fishing fleet. Although they were cautiously polite, they refused to tell anyone what they were looking for.

Two Seals came aboard carrying short-stock M-16s. The al-Husaynis pretended they didn't understand English, so one of the Seals attempted some very elementary Arabic.

Ibrahim invited him to inspect the boat's cabin. Fortunately the Seal showed little interest in the foul-smelling fish hold where Jack and Hasan, stripped to their shorts, were hiding in uncomfortable intimacy with some dead sharks.

The Americans questioned the brothers about their communications gear—surprising in these waters—and radioed the Yemeni authorities to check the boat's identity, and it was rapidly confirmed that the al-Husaynis were pillars of the fishing fleet. The Americans apologized, shook hands, and sped away.

Ten minutes later, as Jack and Hasan emerged from the hold, Jalal held his nose in mock shock at their new perfume. Jack and Hasan took turns dumping water buckets over each other's head until the stench finally was diluted to a tolerable level.

Hasan was inconsolable over the incarceration of his wife and their baby, and talked little. His adopted country had slapped him in the face, and he no longer even made jokes about the Mets—what was the point?

Jack, meanwhile, wished he really could call his best friend, Sebastian Chen, to the rescue, as Sebastian had offered back in

California. Absentmindedly he said to Jalal, "You guys have been terrific, but too bad you don't have a phone." He meant it as a joke.

"Who says we don't have a phone?" replied Jalal. "Wait a minute." He went below and reemerged with a brand new Neva Worldphone. "Bought it from a pirate," he confessed sheepishly.

Jack's eyes bugged out. "Can I make a call? I mean, does it work?"

"Absolutely. We use it to talk to Muhammed and our wives."

"But can I phone the States?"

"Why not? Just charge it to al-Husayni Ltd." Jalal laughed.

They were entering the tiny harbor at Qaysoh before they could finally figure out all the codes necessary to call Pasadena. The phone rang for a minute.

"Who the heck is this?" Sebastian was groggy and irate. It was about 3 A.M. Pacific Standard Time.

"Batman."

"Jack! Boy, we've been worried about you. Lucy asks about you every day. Are you in trouble?"

"More trouble than you can possibly imagine."

"Hey bro, I can be at LAX in an hour . . ."

Jack interrupted Sebastian. "No, I need help of another kind—it might save our lives. Remember that time we talked about your father? Remind me again who he works for . . ."

CHAPTER ELEVEN: *Enter the Dragons*

The serpent is the ruler of the Island and the king of the Land of Punt,
the Frankincense Country. The name of the Island, he says, is Pa-anch, the Isle of
the Genii, and it is inhabited by seventy-five other serpents and one young girl.
ANCIENT EGYPTIAN DESCRIPTION OF SOCOTRA[23]

Other legends speak of people being eaten by a giant serpent, and we recorded
one legend that to a remarkable degree echoed a well-known Near Eastern myth
about a serpent. Even today on Socotra one occasionally hears a story
about somebody who has seen a huge serpent that eats goats and sheep.
VITALY NAUMKIN[24]

*J*ulia felt as if her feet were glued to the cave floor. She was just too horrified to walk over and look at the hideous skull that Conor was holding, so he brought it to her.

"What do you think? Looks like an adult."

Weasel snarled at it from his pouch.

Julia snapped back into action. "Yeah, some of the teeth seem to be missing. Let's look at the other bones."

She showed Conor a crushed femur.

"Imagine the jaws that did that." He shivered.

"Do you want to turn back?"

"It's up to you—you still have an hour of exploration time left." Conor grinned.

Julia shone her flashlight toward the waters ahead. "Let's go on a little further, but stay close. You too, Weasel."

They proceeded warily. As the tunnel expanded into a large, vaulted hall, the noise was terrific. A small river cascaded into cave from a twenty-by-ten-foot opening. It fell fifteen feet into a swirling whirlpool that seemed to suck the water straight down to the center of the earth. The only passageway was a rather treacherous ledge behind the falls, leading to a rubble pile on the far side of the water.

In the beams of their flashlights they could see two passageways beyond the breakdown: one plunged downward, while the other rose steeply.

"Might be an exit," suggested Conor.

"Worth the risk of traversing the waterfall?" asked Julia.

"Let me go first." Conor proceeded cautiously, inserting some chocks and nuts in the wall behind the falls for safe handholds. Even so, Julia had difficult keeping her balance on the ledge, which had been polished so smooth by the action of the water that it might have been lubricated with oil. One slip and she would immediately disappear forever into the black maelstrom.

Conor, as usual, seemed to have no problem, so Julia decided to conceal her anxiety.

"OK, Julia?" he asked.

"Watch out for yourself, flatfoot," she kidded.

Finally they climbed to safety on top of the rubble pile.

"Julia, shine your light up that chute."

Once again their hopes were crushed: the passageway ended after about thirty feet.

"OK, let's see what's down that hole," said Conor.

It was a miniature version of the Devil's Staircase. They left their duffels containing the scuba gear on the rubble pile and proceeded to climb down into the Stygian gloom.

63. THE BLACK LAKE

At the bottom was a large, seemingly bottomless black lake. Scores of stalactites hung from the ceiling, almost touching the velvet surface of the lake. At the far end, perhaps one hundred and fifty feet away, the ceiling came within a few inches of the water.

"Dead end?" asked Julia somberly.

"I don't know; there's something strange here. Turn your light off."

"You're kidding."

"No. I need total darkness."

Julia reluctantly turned off her headlamp and flashlight as Conor extinguished his carbide miner's lamp. It seemed a foolish thing to do: the only thing they knew of to deter the salamanders was the animal's hypersensitivity to bright light. In the dark, Conor and Julia became vulnerable prey.

"Conor, this makes me nervous. What are you up to?"

"Give me a minute. Our eyes need to adjust to the dark."

She waited anxiously. Suddenly she became aware of a very faint bluish glow that illuminated the tiny airspace at the far end of the lake.

"My god, what's that?"

"Light."

"I know, dumbo, but where's it coming from? Phosphorescent organisms or chemicals in the water?"

"Could be, but I prefer to think it's actually sunlight—there must be a shaft or large crack to the surface. Let's turn our lights back on."

Now they were blinded by the glare, so they waited another minute for their eyes to readjust to the brightness.

"We need to explore the end of the lake and find out where the light is coming from."

"Conor, this will be a tricky swim," Julia cautioned. "There's almost no air space toward the far end."

"Let's go back and get the scuba gear. If there is a chute or crack at the end of the lake that we can climb, we're saved; otherwise, we retrace our steps."

Julia gazed at the surface of the black lake. It was absolutely still, then a few large air bubbles broke the surface.

"Might just be carbon dioxide," suggested Conor. "Or maybe those little fish."

"Might be a monster," replied Julia.

64. THE ATTACK

They decided to go whole hog and put on wetsuits. Their pony tanks of air were good for ten or fifteen minutes, enough for several round-trips across the lake. They checked each others' gear and adjusted their valves.

Julia was worried about Weasel. She tried to make him stay behind on the bank, but he insisted on following her into the water, so she reluctantly let him swim along.

The shallow rim quickly gave way to an abyss—indeed, the lake was shockingly deep. After ten or twenty feet, the light from their headlamps simply diffused into the gloom. There was no evidence of a bottom.

Conor frog-kicked away from Julia and she followed. Despite her wetsuit, the cold soon made her bones ache.

A few fish darted by, and Weasel chased and caught one. He surfaced and floated on his back, enjoying a leisurely snack.

Conor was already halfway across, just a few feet under the water, when Julia suddenly saw another trail of bubbles. They weren't from Conor. She switched into a desperate breaststroke.

She was just a few feet or so behind Conor when she saw something—hideously pink and ghastly white—coming at him from below.

Julia grabbed Conor's ankle, and he spun around in a half-sitting stance. She swam up, facing him, and grasped his shoulders, putting herself deliberately in the path of the attack.

The salamander hit her upper back hard enough to knock her mouthpiece out, but it did not bite her. It swam to the surface, then dived straight down, out of sight.

After Conor quickly helped Julia put her mouthpiece back in, he tried to turn her around to shield her, but she strong-armed him and shook her head. They wrestled for a moment, each vying to protect the other.

Then Conor's eyes lit up with horror, and he motioned for Julia to look down: three huge pale forms were rapidly swimming toward them.

Julia, with every ounce of her strength, pushed Conor forward, forcing him to swim for the far shore. She followed as fast as she could. Every time he attempted to turn back toward her, she gestured wildly for him to keep swimming, and he reluctantly obeyed.

They were both braced for an imminent attack, but none came. Julia thought perhaps the salamanders had retreated.

Then she looked to her side, right into shallow, empty eyesockets. The creature was a monstrous albino with a flat, larval head and a huge broad mouth filled with tiny, razor-sharp teeth. Its body, fully six feet long, was almost transparent, with pink frilly gills and grotesquely visible internal organs.

She felt something gently nudge her from the other side—it was another salamander. She sensed a third was right behind her.

Yet she suddenly realized that she was not in acute danger: it had to be because of Tatra's amulet, which somehow protected her. The salamanders were, however, about to devour Conor.

She unzipped the neck of her wetsuit and yanked off the moon amulet. As she thrust it in the direction of one of the salamanders, it immediately recoiled.

Conor simultaneously turned around, thinking Julia was under attack, so he swam toward her just as the second salamander lunged toward him. Julia frog-kicked between them with the amulet in her outstretched fist. Even though the salamander's mouth was open, just inches away from Conor's thigh, it didn't bite him—it simply froze in a kind of confused stupor.

Julia clung to Conor's back and prodded him sharply with her knees, just as if she were forcing a horse to gallop. He immediately understood that she was trying to use the amulet to protect both of them. They both kicked as hard as they could. The far shore of the lake was now only a few feet away.

The salamanders repeatedly attempted to bite at them, but Julia deftly managed to counter their thrusts with the power of the amulet. She felt absurdly like one of those ludicrous figures in a horror film using a cross to duel with a vampire.

They reached the shore and hoisted themselves out of the water. Weasel, miraculously, was already waiting for them. Julia slipped from Conor's back, and for a moment they were separated.

Suddenly a salamander lurched from the water and attacked Conor, and blood spurted from his ankle. The salamander started to take a second bite when Weasel counterattacked.

The brave little civet cat sank his teeth into one of the salamander's gills. The huge creature writhed and twisted, but it was unable to shake free of Weasel's determined jaws; it backed away from Conor toward the water. It emitted a shrill cry, and its two siblings surfaced ferociously.

One snapped its jaws around Weasel. Instantly, Julia threw herself at the salamanders, screaming and beating them with her fists, one of which still clenched the moon amulet. Despite his wound, Conor joined the attack with a large rock.

The salamanders retreated into the black water, one of them with Weasel's broken little body in its jaws.

65. THE LAST OPTION

Julia's brave civet had saved Conor's life, and he wept along with her as he cradled her head. Something stirred again in the lake. They had to move to safety.

Leaving their scuba tanks and a trail of blood, they climbed to a ledge about fifteen feet above the lake, at the mouth of a steeply angled chute.

Conor grabbed Julia and turned her head upward. There was a weak shaft of light coming from far above. "Our exit from this nightmare."

Julia, tears streaming down her cheeks, nodded. Then she unclipped her first-aid kit from her diving belt and started to dress Conor's wound. He was bleeding profusely, but the bite wasn't deep enough to sever a tendon or require a suture.

"There—you'll live," she advised.

He stroked her head. "The salamanders are afraid of you. Perhaps you're a witch after all."

Julia struggled to regain her composure, putting her science hat back on.

"The salamanders sense the magnetism of the meteoritic amulet; that's Tatra's real magic. Somehow they've learned to associate magnetism with pain or danger—Pavlovian conditioning, perhaps. In any event, it deters them."

"But you didn't know that for sure. You took an insane risk under the water to defend me—you easily could've been torn to pieces."

"It didn't matter at the time," said Julia. "Anyway, it's your problem if you can't accept being saved by a woman, macho man."

Conor smiled. "Thank you for saving my life."

"Thank poor Weasel," Julia started to sob again, and Conor hugged her. Again there was a noise from below.

"Damn it," said Julia. She removed her diving light from its headband, and holding it in her hand, shone it downwards. "They're trying to climb up."

Conor quickly aimed his light at the salamanders as well. He kicked down a few rocks for good measure.

The creatures quickly retreated, but not all the way to the water. They squatted next to the abandoned scuba tanks, waiting, while their weak lungs gasped for air and their now useless gills fluttered nervously on the sides of their enormous heads. They looked upwards, eyelessly, toward their prey.

Julia pondered the situation.

"There's a definite zone of discomfort," she observed. "But after about fifteen feet the light is too weak to cause them much pain. Likewise, this weak natural light doesn't seem to bother them. In a few hours our batteries will be dead. What will we do then?"

"Swim back across the lake for our carbide lights and photo flashes?"

"Idiot," she scolded.

"Then our only option is to climb out now." Conor peered upward. "Looks like a classic chimney—even a gym yuppie like you should be able to climb it."

Julia gave him a mock sneer, then became more serious. "Will your ankle be OK?"

"Probably. But if not, you can carry me out, Superwoman."

66. CLIMBING FOR DEAR LIFE

They climbed barefoot in their wetsuits. Conor used the rest of the bandages in the first-aid kit to wrap the middles of their feet. "A little extra traction," he reassured Julia.

The first one hundred feet was a simple exercise in chimneying: the chute was narrow enough that they could brace their backs against one wall and their feet straight against the other. From this position, it was easy to ratchet upwards by bending one leg back, planting a foot against the back wall, standing partially up, bringing the back leg straight to the forewall again, and repeating.

At the top there was a ledge, and the chute became a steep incline for another one hundred and fifty feet which could be walked in a careful crouch. The floor was littered with oozing larvae and their crunchy cocoons.

Julia scooped up a handful of the slithering forms. "Locusts."

"Ecological mystery solved," Conor smiled. "Zillions of locusts hibernate in the cool moist cracks of the karst."

Julia finished his thought. "And some fall down into the subterranean streams and deep sumps where the blind cave fish eat them."

"And the salamanders eat the cave fish." Conor offered Julia an energy bar. They squeezed around a breakdown and saw bright sunlight on the walls ahead.

Their initial joy was tempered, however, when they reached the bright circle of light. Above them, to be sure, was blue sky, but the hole was too big.

"Looks like a mine shaft," said Julia, as she turned off her light. "Maybe one hundred feet high?"

"Try two hundred," suggested Conor. "A ten-story building to you."

"Can we climb it?" Julia saw no obvious route. The shaft was squarish and the walls had cracks and handholds, but they also had overhangs and polished knobs that would be extremely difficult to surmount.

Julia pointed to the largest crack. "Should we jam that?"

Conor was lost in intense study of the problem.

"Conor?"

"No, Julia, not that way. The crack runs out two-thirds of the way up; the traverse to the next crack would be too dangerous. It's safer to tackle the dihedral." Conor pointed to an almost right-angled corner that rose with little variation to an overhang near the top.

"We can stem the whole route. Just a little circus acrobatics to get past the overhang, and we're in the clover." His voice was calm and determined. ("Stemming" is a bridge technique that uses the counterpressure of the feet and hands on intersecting walls. The wider the angle of the walls, the greater the difficulty.)

Julia surveyed the proposed route and shook her head. "I defer to your expertise, but that's an incredibly wide angle. I'm not sure I have the experience to climb it unprotected."

"Who says you'll be unprotected?" Conor smiled.

Julia was annoyed. "Well, what do you propose for protection? Tie our wetsuits together and bite into rock with our teeth?"

"Calm down. You lead, I'll be just below you in wedged-for-dear-life position. Believe me, I'll be a secure platform. If you have any problem, use my head or shoulders."

Julia could hardly believe what Conor was proposing. On the other hand, she couldn't think of a better alternative.

"Buck up—I won't let you fall." Conor's eyes twinkled.

Like Jack, Julia was often amazed by Conor's seemingly boundless reserves of humor in the most dire or unhappy circumstances. But it gave her confidence.

"OK, General, I'll start climbing."

"Let me give you a boost." Conor leaned against the wall diagonally, and Julia, a competitive gymnast in high school, bounded up his back and onto the dihedral.

"Remember, Julia," Conor coached, "stemming is all about balance and flexibility. And you have superb assets."

In theory, Conor was right, but Julia was inexperienced, and the cost was rapid fatigue. She strained too much, especially with her upper-arm muscles, afraid to loosen the tension that held her in place.

Conor, on the other hand, was maddeningly supple and nonchalant. He knew how to coil like a spring, then with an ingenious hand or leg motion, ratchet himself a few feet higher. He could see that Julia was quickly tiring.

They were about eighty feet up the corner, high enough to die if they fell.

"Julia, gently step back and stand on my shoulder. You need to rest."

"Conor, you're crazy." Julia sounded winded.

"No, my knee is locked against the wall. I could hold three of you here for an hour."

She gingerly felt for his shoulder with one foot and then another. She took some deep breaths.

"Now see how well that worked?" Conor was soothing. "From here on out, we'll climb like a caterpillar. I want you to keep at least one foot on my shoulder. We'll talk out each move, OK?"

Julia relaxed. "OK, I *am* better; I was cramping up. Let's go: there's a short crack in the left wall. I'm going to jam it with my fist, then brace my leg."

"Go for it."

Julia quickly gained another fifteen feet, with Conor right behind her. Another brief rest, another few feet.

Ten minutes later they arrived at the crux of the climb: the overhang.

67. THE MONSTER'S BOYFRIEND

"Conor, this scares the hell out of me." Julia tensed.

"No it doesn't—you've got nerves of steel. Look at what you've just climbed."

Julia looked down the almost sheer wall to the tiny patch of light far below.

"5.11, maybe even 5.12. Julia, you're a monster."

She did feel a swell of pride. "OK, then what are you?"

"The monster's boyfriend?" he offered meekly.

"Might be a possibility if you can get us past this overhang."

"Well, just have a seat." Conor pointed to a tiny ledge with a nearby crack for a secure handhold about six feet below the top of the overhang. After she easily reached the bench and sat down, she offered a hand to Conor.

"No thanks, I'm fine where I am." He was relaxed in a perfect "bridge" position. "But take off your wetsuit."

"You're joking."

"Why not? We can knot them together and have almost ten feet of safety line."

With a single free hand, it took Julia nearly five minutes to get out of the wetsuit. Wearing only a swimsuit, she shivered in the sudden cold. She carefully stood up and handed the wetsuit to Conor.

She shook her head at him. "I won't bother to ask if you're wearing anything under yours."

"Yeah, don't ask." He smiled. He knotted her wetsuit around his waist and began to test the rock above him.

Julia's stomach knotted as Conor reached up and then twisted his body around into the classic "Egyptian." He swung loose, cross-hooked his hands, and was on the lip of the overhang with a leg dangling free. Julia clenched her fists. Conor smoothly powered up, then mantled to the top.

Julia clapped. "Now how do you propose to get me over that?"

A minute later Conor lowered down the two wetsuits securely tied together.

"The fabric will stretch but it won't break. Tie each of the legs around and under your arms. . . . That's right. Now stand up."

Julia looked down again, then gritted her teeth. Conor was hanging as far over the edge as possible, with one of his knees locked securely in a deep horizontal crack.

"Will it hold me?" Julia asked.

"Believe," he replied.

And she did. She pulled back on the wetsuit belay to about thirty degrees to give her feet positive traction on the wall. For a moment she was hung suspended over the abyss, then she found one handhold and then another. She felt the knot unraveling under one arm, but she didn't panic; instead she emulated Conor's technique and managed to pull off a partial "Egyptian" herself.

She vaulted the final few feet and collapsed next to Conor, who quickly covered himself with the wetsuits.

Julia laughed, turning her head, as Conor untied the suits and snuggled back into his.

They sat on the ledge just a short crawl from the mouth of the hole and the plateau itself.

For the first time they noticed that their hands and feet, reduced to hamburger meat, were bleeding from scores of cuts.

They held their hands up and laughed.

"Battle wounds," said Julia.

"Stigmata of saints," Conor quipped back.

"You saved me," said Julia.

"No, stupid, you saved me," Conor gushed back.

"I suppose we saved each other, and Weasel saved us both," Julia said quietly.

"I don't know about you, but I'm famished."

Conor offered Julia a hand, and together they climbed out of the Socotran underworld.

CHAPTER TWELVE: *Prisoners of War*

For defensive reasons, the islanders took to sorcery, and when the late
twelfth-century Ayyubids sailed for Suqutra with five warships,
the Suqutris magicked their island out of sight. For five days and nights
the Ayyubid fleet quartered the seas, but found no trace of it.

IBN AL-MUJAWIR (1407)[25]

68. HOWDY

*J*ulia looked up gratefully toward the sun—instead she saw a huge figure in khaki combat fatigues.

"Howdy, little lady."

Colonel Strong, wearing his usual sinister dark glasses and huge grin, was standing with his arms crossed over his chest. Half a dozen other U.S. soldiers wearing tan desert uniforms were gathered around an ominous-looking military helicopter.

Strong pointed to the Black Hawk. "Delta Air Lines at your convenience. Coffee, tea, or milk?"

Conor had no time for the cute humor. "My brother and Dr. Hasan were captured by Kaitos. Do you have any word of them?"

Strong's frown darkened the ground in front of him. "No, I was kinda hoping you could tell me where they were."

Julia, still shivering in her wetsuit, briefly explained how they were deliberately stranded by the pirates and had barely managed the dangerous climb out of the cave. She didn't mention the salamanders.

Strong hardly seemed to listen. "So where's that little varmint of yours, Miss Julia?"

"If you mean my pet civet, he died." Julia grimaced.

"Boo-hoo," said Strong disdainfully.

"You're despicable," Julia spat back.

Strong smiled. "And you're my prisoners."

69. THE BULLY

The Black Hawk flew them back to the Delta Force compound at the airfield. The perimeter was guarded by Yemenis, but only Americans and their captives were allowed inside.

Conor and Julia were first given a medical inspection. "What the hell bit you?" the medic asked Conor.

"Cut myself on a serrated stalactite," Conor fibbed.

The medic shrugged his shoulders. "Could've fooled me. Looks like an alligator tried to kiss you."

The kids were allowed to take showers and change into stiff, oversized military fatigues. They were led into a small office with a desk, conference table, and chairs. One of the American commandos offered them some coffee.

"Did you bring Starbucks with you?" Julia was pleasantly surprised by the quality, although Conor would have preferred a cup of Bewley's.

"Where you from, miss?" asked the tall soldier, with a trace of a Spanish accent.

"I go to Columbia University, but I grew up in the East Village. Do you know Manhattan?"

"Hey, *guapa*, I'm a Dominicano from Washington Heights," he laughed.

"And you, little bro." He focused on Conor. "Let me guess where your accent's from. Hell's Kitchen? Inman? Fordham Road?"

Conor was baffled, but Julia giggled.

"No, he's real Irish."

"No kiddin'," smiled the soldier. "The 'ould sod,' huh? Know any leprechauns?"

"Loads," said Conor, relaxed by the friendly demeanor of the young American. Then the door opened.

"What is this, a hippie love-in?" barked a familiar voice.

"Sir!" The young soldier instantly froze to attention. Colonel Strong gave him a withering look.

"These two are not your Sesame Street playmates, they're prisoners. Out of here, Hernandez, on the double!"

The soldier blushed, saluted, and immediately left the room. Two other soldiers, older and more menacing, entered. They closed the door and assumed the "at ease" position with their arms behind their backs.

"Sit down," Strong ordered Julia and Conor.

Julia started to obey, but then noticed that Conor hadn't moved. She stood up again.

"I told you to sit down," Strong repeated.

Conor stared calmly into the angry blue eyes of his captor. While the salamanders had been scary, this petty tyrant wasn't.

"No—we're tired of being bullied around. Tell us first what you are doing to find my brother and Hasan."

Strong signaled the two guards. One stood immediately behind Julia, the other behind Conor. Strong got up and circled around them; there was imminent violence in his movements. Then suddenly he relaxed.

"Come outside with me for a moment." He smiled at Conor. The guard placed his hand on Conor's shoulder, but Conor didn't flinch or take his eyes away from Strong.

The guard pushed him toward the door, and he didn't resist. Julia started to go with him, but she was held back.

Conor was led down the corridor of the prefabricated barracks and out into a little courtyard. The wind was kicking up some dust, and it was growing colder.

Strong pointed to a dismal pile of goat droppings.

"Do you know what that is?" he asked Conor, who refused to respond. "That's your future if you ever defy me again."

"Oh, I thought it was your lunch," Conor quipped.

The guard grasped Conor in a headlock while Strong shot a fist into his solar plexus. Conor doubled up and gasped for air, but he refused to cry out. The guard released his grip and pushed Conor into the dirt.

Strong bent over him. "Want to go another round, Paddy boy?"

To Strong's surprise, Conor laughed defiantly. "Any Northsider in Dublin can throw a better sucker punch than you, Colonel."

Strong furrowed his brow. "Do you have any idea what I can do to you?"

Conor got up, dusted himself off, and shrugged his shoulders. "Do what you wish," he said fiercely. "But you won't get anything out of me until you help find my brother."

Strong seemed first confused, then annoyed by Conor's reaction.

"Throw this one in the hole," he ordered the guard. "If he wants to play the tough *hombre*, I'll talk to his girlfriend instead."

70. JULIA'S "BACKGROUND"

"Where's Conor?" Julia demanded.

"I've put loudmouth in the box for a few hours. He's lucky I didn't string him up by his goolies."

"Well, you can put me in the box as well." Julia was seething. "I don't cooperate with fascists."

"Fascist?" Strong was suddenly excited. "Isn't that a Commie term? Are you a Marxist, Miss Julia? A Party member?"

Julia rolled her eyes. "No, I'm a biologist. And for your information, a 'fascist' is a bullying ignoramus in a uniform who thinks he can ride roughshod over other people's rights."

"Why, I take that as a compliment," said Strong. "'Cept I don't think terrorists and their sympathizers have any so-called 'rights.'"

"I'm sick of this," said Julia.

"Ah, come on now, I'm enjoying our little conversation." Strong snickered. "I mean, you really fascinate me."

"In what regard?" said Julia coldly.

"Well, for one thing, you're a Jew, aren't you?"

Julia could anticipate what was coming next. "Yes, I am a Jew. And a New Yorker, and a feminist, and a scientist, and an environmentalist, and a lot of other things you probably despise or don't understand."

"Whoa," said Strong. "I'm all for the Jews. The Israeli Army is top-notch—love those boys and girls. Our best allies."

Julia just stared at him. She realized she could probably have a more intelligent conversation with one of the salamanders.

"But what I don't get," Strong said as he scratched his head for emphasis, "is why a Jewish kid would be hanging out with all these Palestinian and Arab fanatics."

"Fanatics? Are you talking about my advisor, Dr. Hasan, and Samira, my best friend?"

"Ah, come on, kid. Yeah—those two and Anwar, the old revolutionary. You must hate your parents and background a lot to join the other side. Or do they give you drugs or something?"

Julia stood up and said quietly, "In respect to my parents, whom I love very much, and for the sake of what you call my 'background,' here's a little Hebrew expression to end our conversation with: *Litznoach ve'lamoot!*"

Strong chuckled. "Now let me guess . . ."

Jack and Hasan hitched a ride to Hadibo with a fisherman friend of the al-Husaynis. Along the rocky dirt road they passed a Yemeni military patrol lounging in the shade of a small date grove. Jack slid down in the seat until they were out of sight.

The fisherman dropped them off in a back street of Socotra's dusty little capital. He warned that a large contingent of new troops from the mainland, along with some more Americans, had flown in the day before. The local people, used to being left to their own devices, were unhappy with the enhanced military presence, especially the arrogant *nasranis*. There were rumors that the Americans were searching for some lost treasure.

Jack started toward the wide main street.

"No, Jack, the street is too dangerous. This way." Hasan pointed to a narrow alley behind the little *suq*.

At the end of the fetid alley, full of decaying fruit and biting flies, Hasan very cautiously peered around the corner, looking for a military patrol.

"Coast is clear. Let's run for it."

They darted out of the alley, ran down a wide dirt street, and turned up another. An elderly fishmonger grinned as they ran past. She had no teeth.

A dirt-splattered Land Rover was parked in front of the pink two-story mud-brick compound that served as the United Nations developmental and scientific headquarters for Socotra. Jack and Hasan bolted for the door.

Inside they nearly knocked over Michele, the young Frenchwoman who administered the sustainable fisheries program.

"Dr. Hasan! We've been so worried about you," she exclaimed.

Hasan grabbed her arm. "Michele, where are Samira, Omar, the others . . ."

"*Très terrible*, Doctor." Michele had tears in the corners of her eyes. "They were arrested and taken to the barracks. Now we've heard they're being moved to the American camp at the airport."

Hasan was stunned. "But why, Michele, *pourquoi?*"

"We still don't know. No one will tell us why they are being detained. Or, for that matter, why they have arrested your two young colleagues."

"Conor and Julia?" Jack was elated that they were safe, even if they were in a military dungeon.

"*Oui*, the Americans found them yesterday. And now I am afraid they are looking for you." Michele sounded frightened.

"But Michele, what does San'a say? Have you contacted Geneva?" Hasan was asking about the UN higher command.

"Most surely. In fact, Harmsen just arrived."

Jack remembered the polite but ineffectual UN representative from the initial confrontation with Colonel Strong at the airport.

Just then Harmsen came through the door.

"Hasan, Jack—my god, you're safe!"

"Hi, Gert," Hasan said as he embraced Harmsen. Jack shook his hand.

"Why are we being hunted down like terrorists?" Jack asked.

"Probably a huge misunderstanding. You should never have visited that so-called witch at Ras Momi. She's Kaitos's sister, and now the Americans think you have something to do with him."

"In fact, we were his prisoners for several days." Hasan gave Harmsen, who seemed horrified, a brief account of their adventure, but he didn't mention the atomic device.

"Did you see anything unusual in Kaitos's hideout?" Harmsen asked.

"Like what?"

"I don't know, but the rumor is that he stole something of immense value from the Greek freighter he blew up."

"Kaitos didn't blow up any freighter," Jack interjected.

"Oh yes, Jack, I'm afraid he did," said Harmsen. "It's world news— the entire crew died. Yesterday the American Secretary of State held a press conference to announce that the war on terrorism was now also a war on piracy. He mentioned Kaitos by name. This has very big international complications, especially for our UN programs here in Socotra. We will be horribly compromised by any connection, however innocent or unintentional, with local piracy."

Jack looked at Hasan, who was scowling.

"Gert, have you seen Samira?" Hasan changed the subject.

"Oh yes, Hasan, she and the baby are fine. You shouldn't worry."

"How about Anwar, Hadad, Tariq?" Hasan asked.

"I'm afraid Hadad is also in custody. Anwar was released but then rearrested. Tariq is hiding somewhere; they claim he is trying to organize an Islamic guerrilla movement in the mountains. They say he is affiliated with al-Qaeda and other terrorist groups."

"Tariq?" Hasan was incredulous. "That's preposterous!"

"Perhaps. But it is another part of our dilemma here. The Americans have practically accused us of providing cover for pirates and terrorists."

"Well, Gert," Hasan said sharply, "what have you done to defend us? These charges are the ravings of lunatics."

"Please calm down, Hasan." Harmsen seemed shaken. "We're doing our best. In fact, I am just waiting for a call from the Secretary-General's office. Can you excuse me for a few minutes?"

"OK, but please, Gert, get the old man to show some backbone. This whole affair is absurd."

Harmsen went out. Michele made some tea for Jack and Hasan. About fifteen minutes went by.

"Hasan, come here, *vitement!*" Michele was at the window. "The rat," she said angrily. "Gert's betrayed you."

The UN compound was completely encircled by Yemeni Special Forces troops, and they could see Harmsen talking to someone in a Humvee with U.S. insignia: the ubiquitous Colonel Strong.

72. REUNION

The Americans locked Conor in a tiny underground cubicle bigger than a breadbox but smaller than a cellar. He wouldn't have minded catching a few winks, but he was too hungry to fall asleep, and besides, he was sharing the space with a rather ill-tempered scorpion.

The scorpion—which, for all Conor knew, might be a fatally poisonous species—dueled for a while with Conor's finger (wrapped in a sock), then retreated to its own hole. This gave Conor some quiet time to think about rescuing Jack and Hasan. His best bet, he thought, was to break out of the compound and try to reach the UN office in Hadibo.

After a few hours, the young soldier from New York released Conor from his claustrophobia. While he didn't speak to the soldier for fear of getting him in more trouble, he instead gave an experimental wink. The soldier smiled back furtively.

Strong was nowhere to be seen. A bald lieutenant who failed to introduce himself told Conor that he could wait with "a few friends" until interrogation resumed. Conor asked about Julia, but the officer ignored him.

The friendly soldier escorted him down the hall. "She's OK," he said softly. "I just gave her some rations. She's worried about you, but I'll get word that you're still in one piece."

"Thanks, mate." Conor was again touched by the soldier's kindness.

"And now a big surprise," whispered the soldier as he opened the door.

"Ya bowsie," shouted Jack. "So the dragons didn't eat you after all."

"Oh, ya plonker," cried Conor as he rushed to embrace his big brother. Hasan joined the scrum. The soldier smiled and locked the door.

"Any idea how worried I've been about you?" said Jack.

"Worried about me? Why, you big sod, you're the one was captured by pirates."

Jack suddenly looked grave and whispered in Conor's ear. "The room is probably bugged; that's why they've put us together. Be careful what you say."

Conor pointed to some paper and pen on a desk.

Jack again whispered in his ear. "They think we're idiots. If you write something, eat it." Conor nodded.

They chatted in low voices—why make the eavesdroppers' work easy? Hasan told Conor how they were betrayed by Harmsen. Conor frowned.

"OK, Superman, time to share and tell." Jack smiled at Conor.

"You first, Batman."

"No, you," said Hasan as he clamped a friendly hand on Conor's shoulder.

Conor grinned. He saw no reason to censor the details for Strong's sake; he wouldn't believe the part about the salamanders anyway. So he launched into the tale of the labyrinth, Julia's incredible bravery, and Weasel's heroic sacrifice.

Jack and Hasan were spellbound. Julia's conjecture about the salamanders was now an incredible scientific discovery. Moreover, the existence of the Socotran "dragons" would be a huge new argument for making the island a world biosphere reserve.

"Wow," gasped Hasan as Conor finished his tale (during which he had greatly understated his own climbing feats).

"OK," said Conor. "Your turn."

Jack and Hasan proceeded cautiously, telling much of the story but not giving away the location of Kaitos's hideaway—"We were blindfolded and don't know where we landed; perhaps near Ras Momi"—or the secret of the Russian bomb.

While Hasan was talking, Jack tore off a piece of paper and wrote: "The Yanks sank the freighter. With all hands." He showed it to Conor, who looked shocked, then Jack swallowed the note as Hasan continued to talk into the hidden microphone.

A little later, while Jack was talking about the speedboats, Hasan wrote: "Kaitos stole two attaché cases from the freighter. It's a Russian plutonium nuclear device. It is still on the island. We must let the world know about it before it falls into the wrong hands."

He showed the note to Conor, whose jaw dropped. Jack kept up his camouflage talk, and Hasan grimly tore the note into pieces and chewed them like qat. Conor just kept shaking his head.

Jack recaptured Conor's attention with the story of his close encounter with the tiger shark; his brother shivered as Jack described how the shark moved in for the kill, then the sea filled with blood.

"The fisherman's name was Yahya; he and his two brothers saved my life. Also rescued your kayak."

"You're a lucky punter," said Conor in astonishment.

Jack laughed. "Yes, that's what everyone says: 'Lucky man.'"

The door opened. It was the surly lieutenant followed by two of his men.

"We're sponsoring an even bigger family reunion. Grab your gear and come with me."

Conor was surprised to see that Jack had his pack, and he wondered if he still had his magic dust.

73. INDEFINITE DETENTION

They were escorted down the hall, out through the open space, and into another smaller, temporary structure that consisted of a briefing room and an office. On the office door was a small plaque: "Strong, OC/SOP 47, USA."

"Samira!" Hasan was overjoyed to see his wife and baby, along with Anwar and Hadad. Jack was equally excited to see Julia, who was cuddling Omar on her lap. Everyone hugged and exchanged greetings.

Strong came in. He was accompanied by a few soldiers as well as an American civilian, a middle-aged man in a khaki suit who carried a briefcase.

"OK, y'all sit down." Strong glared at Conor. "Unless he-man here wants to stand on his head."

Conor frowned and sat down between Julia and Jack.

The soldiers frisked everyone and did a cursory search of their backpacks and bags. They found Jack's vial of E-dust and the micro-receiver he had borrowed from Caltech.

"What's this?" one soldier asked suspiciously.

Jack smiled nonchalantly. "The tube contains some sparkle I use to identify my microbats, while the electronic apparatus monitors the strength of the microwave beam."

The soldiers were uncomprehending and turned to Strong for guidance.

"Bat sparkle?" The Colonel laughed. "Leave it. Boy genius can keep his toys for now.

"Now listen up!" Strong addressed his prisoners in the same tone with which he ordered his men around. "If you don't cooperate fully with us, this may be the last time you'll ever see each other." He waited to let the threat sink in.

Julia clutched Omar, and Samira grasped her husband's arm. Anwar simply rolled his eyes like the world-weary diplomat he was, while Hadad, Jack, and Conor each shot Strong hateful looks.

"What do you want, Strong?" Anwar asked.

"I want to know where Kaitos is," Strong replied. "I want to know right now."

Hasan was ready to explode with frustration. "But why involve them?" He pointed to the others. "Jack and I are the only ones who have met Kaitos, and we've told you a dozen times that he kidnapped us. We have no idea where he took us. We were blindfolded and terrified."

Strong frowned. "I don't believe that cockamamie story for a second. And even if some of these folks aren't involved in your little cell, their fate is now tied up with yours."

"Cell? Are you implying we're terrorists?" Samira couldn't believe what was going on.

Strong ignored her. "I'm now going to introduce Mr. Mitchell. He represents the Attorney General of the United States."

Anwar whispered a translation to Hadad, who was utterly perplexed by the American threats. "Are we a colony again?" he whispered back.

Mitchell looked both hostile and uncomfortable. "I am with the U.S. Department of Justice. If you don't cooperate fully and immediately with Colonel Strong, you will be put into detention as enemy combatants."

"Enemy combatants!" Samira exploded. "I am an American doctor working for the United Nations. Is the UN the enemy? Or am I an enemy because I come from Brooklyn?"

Mitchell coughed and shifted his feet. "The Secretary-General of the United Nations has been advised of our concerns about links between its staff in Yemen and terrorist groups. If you are detained, you will be transferred to an undisclosed destination and will remain under the control of United States personnel until the President deems otherwise."

"Indefinite detention at Guantanamo Bay, the new Devil's Island?" asked Jack.

Strong laughed. "No, sonny, you got it all wrong—Guantanamo is the Hilton. We got Motel Six plans for your crew."

"Diego Garcia?" asked Anwar, long suspicious that the United States had a secret political prison on its isolated island airbase in the eastern Indian Ocean.

Mitchell glared at him. "Still a Marxist, I presume. Where did you hear about a prison at Diego Garcia? From your Cuban friends?"

Anwar was unruffled. "Is the CIA pretending to be the Department of Justice, or is there no longer any difference?"

All this was totally lost on poor Hadad, and indeed, the exchange between old Cold War enemies was confusing to everyone else as well.

Finally Julia spoke up. "We need to talk about this amongst ourselves. Can you leave us alone for fifteen minutes, without guards or hidden microphones?"

Mitchell looked at Strong, who replied, "Sure, little lady. Mr. Mitchell and I will wait in my office. You have exactly fifteen minutes to decide the rest of your life. The guards are outside, so no funny business. And don't worry about being bugged. I've heard enough tall tales about sharks and salamanders. But remember, this is your last chance: give us Kaitos or kiss your future goodbye."

Strong stationed his men outside and retired to his office with Mitchell.

74. MAGIC, AT LAST

Only a door separated the two groups.

"Strong is probably listening to us," Hasan whispered to the others.

Conor got up and crept close to the door. He put his head on the floor and tried to look through the crack. Then he put his ear to the keyhole.

He came back to the group. "They're arguing about something. I'd really like to know what they're talking about."

"So would I," said Anwar. "We can't formulate any plan of resistance until we understand what this is really all about."

Conor looked at Jack.

"Well, let's listen to their conversation," said Jack softly. Everyone stared at him.

He first took a piece of paper and rolled it into a strawlike tube; then, holding one end with his thumb, from a vial he sprinkled what looked like glitter into the other end. He then went to the door, put the tube up to the keyhole, and blew through the other end.

Everyone, except for Conor, was utterly flabbergasted.

"What did you just do?" Julia demanded.

Jack smiled but refused to answer. He took the "microwave detector" from his pack and very carefully tuned it until Strong's and Mitchell's voices were clearly heard. The group was stunned.

"Caltech E-dust, or 'smart dust,'" Jack explained. "Each speck is a super-miniaturized microphone plus wireless transmitter, hardly bigger than a mote of dust—just a few cubic millimeters; there are optical versions as well. Welcome to the magic age of ultrasmall machines."

Conor beamed with pride at his brother as the others shook their heads in wonder.

"Let's spy on the spies," said Anwar.

CHAPTER THIRTEEN: *Moment of Truth*

The entire world is divided, only people hold it together . . .
TRADITIONAL SOCOTRI SONG[26]

Mitchell glared at his arrogant military counterpart. "Do you really think it was smart to round up such a large group? Harmsen warns that there will be hell to pay from the UN. And four U.S. citizens? It's a media nightmare."

Strong fixed Mitchell coldly with his gaze. "The Pentagon didn't invent this mess—you smart-asses at the Agency did."

Mitchell interrupted him, fuming. "Listen here, Robert, the Army signed off on this plan. This is as much your oil spill as ours."

"Whoa, partner. We agreed only to the original concept: use CIA assets to smuggle a briefcase bomb from Siberia; pretend to be the Russian mafia; lure al-Qaeda with bait they couldn't refuse; close the trap on an island in the Red Sea. But we sure as hell weren't consulted about taking out that freighter."

"Well, what alternative did we have? We couldn't let the device be hijacked, perhaps by bin Laden's men."

Strong smiled like a hunter who has treed a coon. "Well, Wayne, that's more or less what happened. Now if you had let us insert a Delta team on that boat, we wouldn't be in this mess. But no, you insisted that those Russian baby-killers who work for you were as good as my Delta men. And that turned out to be false."

Mitchell smirked. "Well, no point in arguing about it now. Whether you like it or not, the Army is as compromised as the Agency. Unless you want our heads to roll, you better sing with the choir. When we nail Kaitos, we'll celebrate it as a giant victory over a key al-Qaeda operative, and no one will know any better. But we have to get the bomb."

"And leave no witnesses around to tell a different story." Strong pressed the obvious point.

"What now? You want to drop them out of a helicopter?"

"It would be cleaner, Wayne," Strong said diabolically. "'Terminate with extreme prejudice'—I think that's what you guys called it in Nam."

"You know we can't do that," replied Mitchell, without much conviction.

"Then how long do you really think you can keep 'em shut up? Hell, put 'em on Diego Garcia and their mammies will start howling like coyotes. Next thing you know, we got a pack of congressmen on a charter jet to the Indian Ocean."

"Listen, Robert, Diego Garcia is just a scare tactic. The Agency is working on a plan that will thoroughly discredit the whole bunch. We'll get the Yemenis to liquidate their local friends and put that damn Commie Anwar back in prison. We'll strip citizenship from Hasan and young Davis under the Patriot Act and deport them. Ms. Monk will be painted as a self-hating sympathizer with Palestinian extremists, and her friend Samira, a dangerous subversive."

Strong shook his head and laughed. "Wayne, y'all are out of your cotton-pickin' minds. The whole damn Left will make martyrs and heroes out of them—Jesse Jackson gonna be camped in front of your outhouse in Arlington. Give me a break."

Mitchell was sullen and silent.

"Well," said Strong, "if we can't kill 'em, we might as well have us some fun scaring the pants off of 'em."

"Just remember," warned Mitchell, "if we don't find that bomb, this could be bigger than Watergate. Everyone could lose their head, from the President on down to you and me, so you'd better close ranks. We've got to make them tell us where Kaitos's hideout is."

76. DIRTY LITTLE SECRETS

Strong and Mitchell reentered the room. The Colonel also brought in several guards.

"Well, y'all have a nice little heart-to-heart?" Strong smirked.

"No need for that," said Hasan quietly.

"Oh, so you came to your senses and now you're gonna tell me where to find Kaitos. Good boy."

"No, Colonel, we know all your dirty little secrets," Hasan replied levelly.

Mitchell looked worryingly at Strong, who fumed.

"We know who really sank the freighter, and we know why." It was Jack speaking now.

"Don't believe anything Kaitos told you," Strong said defensively.

"No, we heard it from the horse's mouth . . . from you," Jack replied.

Strong looked like fuses were exploding in his brain.

"What the hell are you talking about?" demanded Mitchell.

Jack held up his E-dust receiver. "State of the art, Mr. Mitchell, developed by Caltech. It's a receiver for tiny microphones no bigger than pinheads." He pulled the vial out of his pocket. "We heard your entire conversation."

"Yeah," Samira broke in, "Russian baby-killers, oil spills—the whole sick story."

The two Delta Forces noncoms looked at each other and then at their colonel. He glared back.

"So you better drop us out of a plane quick," added Conor, "before the world learns what complete eejits you two dowsers are."

Strong took a swing at Conor, who easily stepped out of his way. One of the guards leveled his gun at the group.

"Wait a second!" Mitchell was half-afraid that Strong would start massacring the prisoners. "I have no idea what kind of preposterous story you have concocted, but you're our prisoners." He looked over at Strong.

The colonel's eyes were filled with hate. "OK, we're through playing games." He pulled out a nine-millimeter automatic. "On your knees."

Before Conor had a chance to comply, Strong swatted him with the butt of the gun. As Conor dropped, Jack rushed Strong and almost got the barrel of the gun stuck up his nose. Strong smiled demonically as Julia grabbed Jack and pulled him back. Everyone got down on their knees.

"Lawson, get the team!" Strong ordered. Mitchell looked dumbfounded.

A minute later, the room was filled with heavily armed Delta Force men. Everyone except Samira, who was holding Omar, had their hands tied behind their backs. Then they were all hooded, even Samira.

"OK, get 'em outside. You're goin' on a little vacation, ladies and gentlemen," Strong said.

"My baby," Samira cried.

"Don't worry," laughed Strong, "you can take him with you for now. But no promises for the future. If you have a future."

They were led outside where a sharp wind was blowing. In the distance they could hear a plane engine.

They waited—again on their knees—for about a half hour in the courtyard of the compound before being loaded into a truck and driven a short distance.

The kind New York soldier whispered to Julia, "I don't like this, *guapa*. I don't like this at all." He seemed spooked by Strong's behavior.

Julia whispered from underneath her hood. "If anything happens to us, if we disappear, you must let our families know what happened. Strong is a madman."

The soldier squeezed her shoulder as if to reassure her. Meanwhile, little Omar, normally the most sweet-tempered of toddlers, started screaming.

Strong took off Samira's hood so she could comfort her terrified little son.

The truck stopped, and everyone got out. They were parked next to a large transport plane. Oddly, or perhaps ominously, it had no military markings.

The three Humvees with the rest of the military team pulled up in a half circle around the truck. As a soldier started to put the hood back over Samira's head, she shook herself free and shouted, "Look!"

Three or four vehicles were bearing down on them at high speed.

Strong barked an order and a soldier aimed one of the Humvee-mounted M-60 machine guns at the vehicles, which then slowed and cautiously drove towards them.

Several people carrying cameras got out of a jeep. Then another vehicle, a Land Rover, stopped: inside was a television crew.

Mitchell looked like he was going to faint, while Strong just shook his head.

A very distinguished-looking man with Asian features approached the plane; he wore a finely tailored linen suit and carried a notepad. He stared for a second at the pathetic hooded figures.

"Help us!" Samira yelled. "I'm an American citizen. We're being kidnapped."

A soldier put his hand over Samira's mouth, and she bit him. "Ouch!" he yelled, and he looked toward Strong.

"Leave her be," he said coldly.

"Excuse me, officer," said the distinguished man.

"And who the hell do you think you are?" barked Strong.

"My name is Chester Chen. I am the East Asia bureau chief for the *New York Times*, and I'm on special assignment. One of the young men you have hooded and are about to abduct is a classmate of my son."

Strong nervously shifted his feet. "These people are in our custody, and you're interfering with a U.S. military operation."

"Oh, pardon me, Colonel," said Sebastian's dad in a mild but ironic voice. "I thought we were on Yemeni territory. In any event, I bring you some incredible news."

The rest of the press corps now approached, including a cameraman from CNN.

"Turn off the cameras!" yelled Strong.

"Don't you want to hear about the stolen atomic bomb?" Chen asked.

Mitchell looked like he was having a heart attack. The Delta men lowered their weapons, and the New Yorker took off Julia's hood, then those of the others. Strong made no move to stop him.

"What bomb?"

"Well, thanks to that young man," Chen pointed at Jack, "my paper was alerted to a miniature atomic device—actually housed in a briefcase, if you can imagine—left by pirates on an uninhabited island. Just out there." Chen pointed westward.

"Nonsense," said Strong. "This boy is a notorious liar. He and his brother will chew your ear for days with fantastic stories about giant salamanders and killer sharks." Strong spat on the ground.

"Well, in this case, the story was completely true. We've just returned from The Brothers. Two experts from the International Atomic Energy Commission in Geneva accompanied us, and they confirmed it is really a bomb, with Russian markings. And highly dangerous—several of the pirates died of radiation poisoning."

"You left the bomb there?" asked Strong nervously.

"Oh, of course," said Chen, "under guard. We alerted the Yemeni authorities as well as the appropriate UN agencies. Now, if I can introduce my colleagues: we have *Le Monde*, *The Times* of London, the *Washington Post*, CNN, of course, and here . . ."

"Enough!" Strong shouted. "This ain't *Candid Camera*. Now move back, all of you. Take that damn camera outa here!" Strong chased away one of the CNN crew who nonetheless continued to film him.

Mitchell, meanwhile, had hidden himself in one of the Humvees. While Strong and some of his men held the media at bay, other soldiers escorted the prisoners back into the truck. They returned to the compound at high speed, pursued by the press.

Inside the truck, everyone laughed and slapped Jack on the back. "Don't thank me," he said modestly. "Thank my best friend, Sebastian Chen."

78. THE DEAL

Back at the Delta Force compound, the group was divided up into separate rooms: Samira, Julia, and Omar in one; Jack, Conor, and Hasan in another; and Anwar and Hadad in a third. They waited in suspense for several hours, then soldiers brought them some rations and water.

The soldier from New York, who everyone now knew as Corporal Juan Hernandez, told the second trio that all hell had broken loose.

"What do you mean?" asked Conor.

Juan checked his back, then whispered, "Chartered planes are landing every fifteen minutes with more journalists. Strong is throwing tantrums, and Mitchell has disappeared. My sergeant told me to pack, says we're returning stateside within twenty-four hours."

"How about us?" Conor persisted.

"Not a clue, *amigo*. But they ain't going to shoot you in front of CNN." Then he looked at Jack. "Apparently you're the big man on campus now. Strong would like to cut you into ten thousand pieces, but the media says you're a hero." Juan smiled. "Got to go. I may not see you again, but good luck."

"Thanks, Juan. You're a decent bloke," said Conor.

The young soldier left, and Jack saw Hasan smile.

"Feeling better?" asked Jack.

"Much. They can't 'disappear' us, and I don't think they'll prosecute us. Maybe I can see the Mets play next season after all."

"I prefer West Cork," chuckled Conor.

Strong left them alone for the night and everyone tried to catch up on lost sleep. Unfortunately, that was difficult because of the periodic bursts of commotion outside and the continuous coming and going of vehicles.

They were awakened about 6:30 A.M. by a knock on the door.

Conor rubbed sleep out of his eyes. "Since when did Strong become polite enough to knock?"

Hasan got up and tried the door, and it opened. Two middle-aged men in suits stood smiling at him.

"Dr. Hasan?"

"Yes," Hasan replied as he yawned.

"Great pleasure to meet you. I am Ken Abbott, special representative of the Secretary of State, and this is Dwight Hightower, our chargé d'affaires in San'a." They extended their hands.

Hasan introduced Jack and Conor, and the diplomats showered them with smiles and good wishes.

"OK, what's going on?" Jack was suspicious of this unexpected love-fest. "Are we still prisoners of your war on terror?"

"Oh my goodness, no," said Abbott. "Quite the opposite, young man. But if you don't mind, we've brought some breakfast . . . we'd like to talk to your whole team."

They were escorted back to the briefing room where Strong had threatened them the day before. This time there was a buffet with—unbelievably—donuts and scrambled eggs, in addition to Yemeni food.

Julia and Samira were munching on Krispy Kremes. Julia smiled at Jack and Conor.

"We figured you might enjoy an American breakfast," said Hightower. "We had it flown in from the nearby U.S. Naval task force."

Conor winked at Jack. "Well, boyo, this is bleedin' deadly, isn't it?"

Jack whispered, "Yeah, brilliant, but don't trust these mutts for a second—first the bad cops, then the good cops. They're up to something." Conor nodded.

"If I could have your attention, ladies and gentlemen," said Abbott, sounding like the host of a genteel cocktail party. "I know that you have all suffered much mental and emotional stress over the past few days."

Hasan looked at Anwar, who rolled his eyes; Anwar then translated for poor Hadad, who was more confused than ever by the sudden improvement in their fortunes.

"I hope that I can make up for that. I have some very exciting good news to tell you about, but first I want to fill you in on the overall situation." Abbott nodded at Hightower, who in turn walked to the door and talked to someone outside. A naval officer entered.

"This is Commander Hall from Naval Intelligence." The tall officer nodded politely. "He will brief you about the pirate Kaitos and the stolen nuclear weapon."

"Prepare for the worst," Julia whispered to Samira.

"Thank you," said Hall. "Yesterday at 1700 hours our task force located two pirate vessels near Ras Momi. In a brief but very violent engagement, a fast boat unit of Navy SEALS, supported by helicopters from the USS *Vincennes*, killed the pirate Kaitos and all of his associates, including a woman identified as his sister."

Julia clutched at Samira, and Jack shot a horrified look at Conor. "Tatra!"

"On Kaitos's body our SEALS found documents conclusively linking him to the al-Qaeda terror network. As I am sure you have been told, Kaitos—undoubtedly acting on behalf of the terrorists—had conspired to buy a miniaturized nuclear weapon from the Russian mafia. Rather than paying off the Russians, however, Kaitos massacred them and the rest of the crew. Although we were able to track down Kaitos, he had earlier concealed the nuclear device, which was later found by journalists contacted by Mr. Davis and Dr. Hasan."

"Thank you, Commander," Abbott interrupted. The naval officer saluted and left the room.

"Now I must apologize," said Abbott, "for Colonel Strong's earlier misinterpretation of these events. Far from regarding any of you as suspected terrorists, the United States government is proud to acknowledge the heroism of Mr. Davis and Dr. Hasan, and we would like to make suitable amends to the rest of you."

Abbott and Hightower again stood beaming like smiling scarecrows. Jack spoke. "Mr. Abbott, this is a tissue of lies." Hightower frowned, but Abbott kept his sinister smile.

"Kaitos was an indigenous pirate," Jack resumed, "not an 'international terrorist.'" He hijacked the bomb by accident, he had no idea what it was. That's why he kidnapped us, so we could tell him. His men may have killed the Russians—who, incidentally really worked for you—but they certainly did not blow up the Greek freighter. The U.S. Navy did. And Tatra, Kaitos's sister, was our friend. She saved our lives at Ras Momi."

"Sorry, Jack, but all that is past history," said Abbott nonchalantly. "I don't want to get into useless debates with you. Instead, I come here to make you a generous offer. The State Department would like you to meet with the press. We'll understand, of course, if you need to discharge some anger at Colonel Strong and his heavy-handed methods. Believe me, that was totally unauthorized, and Strong has been transferred to lawn maintenance duties at an Army post in Alaska. But we do expect your account of events to jibe with what Commander Hall has just outlined."

Anwar spoke. "Pardon an old diplomat for asking, but what are the rewards for enacting this little charade—and what are the punishments if we refuse?"

"Thank you for being so straightforward." Abbott pretended to chalk figures on an imaginary blackboard. "On one side of the ledger, Davis and Hasan will receive a medal from the President of the United States himself. The UN development program on Socotra will be the recipient of handsome grants from the State Department. Washington will also look favorably on any research proposals that any of you would like to submit in the future. We'd be pleased, for example, to help young Conor here search for mammoths, or fund Samira's well-baby clinics. That's the pot of gold at the end of the rainbow."

"Incredible," said Samira to Julia, who just shook her head in amazement.

"And if we don't cooperate?" asked Anwar.

"The toilet," said Abbott still smiling. "The absolute worst. We won't immediately put you in detention, but we will instigate a comprehensive investigation of possible terrorist ties. Moreover, we'll systematically refute any wild charges you may make concerning the United States government. Your reputations and careers will be in the sewer. And I can't make any promises about the future of noncitizens, especially you, Anwar, with your subversive background. Moreover, your friend Tariq, instead of coming down from the mountains to a comfortable job, will continue to be branded as a guerrilla and will undoubtedly be tracked down by the Yemeni Special Forces."

"Look," interjected Hightower, "don't scowl at us; this is the way the world works. Love it or leave it. We were entirely within our rights to do whatever we could to catch al-Qaeda. I admit, our little scheme self-imploded with some nasty consequences, but you need to keep your eyes on the big picture, the global struggle against terrorism—against evil. Besides, we're not asking you to turn in your mothers, merely act the role of heroes and let the U.S. government provide generous rewards."

Anwar turned and looked at his friends, and then he faced Abbott. "Colonel Strong let us have some time by ourselves to discuss our options. Do you mind leaving for a few minutes?"

Hightower looked nervously at his superior. Abbott shrugged his shoulders. "Look, you're not our prisoners. Of course, take some time to deliberate. But please, ladies and gentlemen, let's not get into an antagonistic frame of mind. We really do want to compensate you generously for your help, as well as for the trouble you have endured. I especially appeal to the four of you who are U.S. citizens. Consider your patriotic duty, please."

The State Department left.

79. THE FIGHTIN' IRISH

As soon as they were alone, Julia pulled out her moon amulet and burst into tears. So, surprisingly, did Conor, and Jack too was on the verge of weeping.

"She saved our lives," Julia said fiercely. "That extraordinary woman. And these liars murdered her to cover up their own dirty conspiracy."

Hasan, meanwhile, was thinking about the pirates. They weren't exactly friends, of course, but he had come to understand what had turned them into brigands. And they were entirely innocent of the preposterous American allegations. He was especially haunted by Kaitos, with his poor shriveled limbs and his magnificent head, his savage temper and his unexpected humanity.

Hasan spoke up. He decided to be the devil's advocate.

"Look, I know how angry you are, but they are also running scared. If we want to haggle, we can probably get Abbott to promise us anything we want, including well-child clinics all over the island and some wonderful research grants for you three kids. We also would be able to protect Anwar, Hadad, and Tariq from recrimination."

Samira exploded from her seat. "One more cowardly sentence, and I swear, I'll divorce you right here and now. How can you talk like this? When you stood up to Strong I was so proud of you, but now you're acting like a worm. Has the truth no meaning for you anymore?"

Julia tried to calm Samira, but she was incandescent.

Hasan smiled. "I knew you'd say that, Samira. You're a fiery woman, and that's why I married you. But how about the rest of you?"

Anwar asked for a moment to explain the situation to Hadad, the one native Socotran in the room. The two men talked for a few minutes, and Hadad became very upset.

"What right do these people," Anwar translated for Hadad, "have to come into my home and order me about? To threaten me with prison one moment and to bribe me with treasure the next? This is our land, and I want nothing more to do with these 'Strongs' or 'Abbotts.'"

"But do you understand the risk, especially to you and Tariq, if we defy them?" Hasan asked in Arabic.

"Have you never read the holy Koran, brother?" replied Hadad. "An honest man does not sell his soul to scoundrels." He was adamant.

"And you, Anwar? This might mean prison, or worse."

"Oh, it would be worth it." Anwar smiled. "My days are probably numbered anyway. But what delight I would take to see them have to eat their lies in front of the entire world."

The old revolutionary chuckled, then became serious. "And remember the poor crew of that freighter, and even Kaitos and his men—they were murdered by these lies."

"OK, kids." Now Hasan turned to the trio.

"I'm fightin' Irish, and so is this big gouger who claims to be my brother," said Conor proudly.

Jack put his arm around him. "The truth," he said quietly. "We must tell absolutely everything."

Hasan looked at Julia. "I suppose I don't even need to ask you, do I?"

Julia, indeed, looked like a warrior queen before battle.

80. THE LAST WORD

Abbott and Hightower returned to hear the verdict.

"We've seen the light," said Julia. "You can take us in front of the cameras now."

Abbott was delighted. "A truly patriotic decision for which I know your government will always be grateful."

Julia and the others smiled back like a pack of Cheshire cats.

Hightower still looked nervous. "There's an incredible swarm of press out there, so please remember your duty."

The group was taken outside where a podium and chairs were already set up. The weather had turned mild and sunny, with an unusually docile wind.

Conor rubbed his eyes in the sunshine. Delta Force was gone, and aside from Abbott's team of half a dozen State Department types, there were mainly Yemeni soldiers and assorted civil servants to orchestrate the historic press conference.

A gate was opened and the media crushed in; there were now almost one hundred members of the press assembled. Kaitos, the bomb, and the UN Speleobiology Project were now the top news in the world.

Sebastian's father walked up and embraced Jack and shook hands with the others. Then he put his arm around Jack and whispered in his ear. "There are rumors of a huge cover-up. I'm sure they've given you the carrot-and-stick treatment, but don't be afraid to tell the whole story: the world is on your side, and Washington is long overdue for an earthquake."

Jack whispered back, "Thanks for everything, Mr. Chen, and brace yourself for some heavy shaking in a few minutes."

Chen looked delighted.

The group had elected Julia to speak on their behalf. First, however,

Abbott and Hightower reread the same press releases that had circulated for the past day. Abbott then praised the remarkable courage of Jack and Hasan, who he called "true American heroes," before he introduced Julia.

She thanked him, and he smiled back. Looking out at the sea of cameras and notepads, Julia blinked a few times, and then reached inside her shirt and pulled out the amulet that Tatra had given her. She held it up.

"This is the symbol of the moon, of the ancient cultures of Socotra, and of the courage of strong women like my friends Tatra and Samira. It is also, for me, a reminder to speak truth always . . ." She turned and fixed Abbott in a steely glare. He shriveled in his seat.

"Everything that Mr. Abbott has just told you is a lie . . ."

Flashbulbs began to pop, and Julia's words turned into shockwaves that would soon rattle a city on the Potomac, thousands of miles away.

In the meantime, Conor thought he could hear something else, faint yet distinct in the hubbub. It sounded like Tatra laughing.

N O T E S (for big kids and science buffs)

1. Cited in Tim Mackintosh-Smith, *Yemen: The Unknown Arabia* (Woodstock, N.Y.: Overlook Press, 2000,) p. 212.

2. James Raymond Wellsted, *Travels to the City of the Caliphs,* vol. 2 (London: H. Colburn, 1840), p. 281.

3. Mackintosh-Smith, *Yemen,* p. 206.

4. See www.nanou.org.

5. *The Periplus of the Erythraean Sea, Travel and Trade in the Indian Ocean, by a Merchant of the First Century* (New York: Longmans, Green, and Co., 1912). Translated from the Greek.

6. Wellsted, *Travels to the City of the Caliphs,* pp. 182, 299.

7. Ibid., p. 266.

8. Socotrans also believe in a vampire demon in the guise of a bat or bird which is called *maleiarid.* See Douglas Botting, *Island of the Dragon's Blood* (New York: Wilfred Funk, 1958,) p. 181.

9. Bent, cited in Botting, *Island of the Dragon's Blood,* p. 220.

10. *The Travels of Marco Polo,* trans. R. E. Latham (London: Penguin, 1958), pp. 296–98.

11. Botting, *Island of the Dragon's Blood,* p. 181.

12. Col. I. E. Snell, *Witch Trials in Socotra* (November 1955, Mukallah), cited in Botting, *Island of the Dragon's Blood,* p. 184.

13. "There was an amazing number of centipedes in this place; we killed fourteen during the evening, and as many on the following morning." Wellsted, *Travels to the City of the Caliphs,* p. 257.

14. Mackintosh-Smith, *Yemen,* pp. 216, 226.

15 ". . . many stories are current of the translation of people into donkeys, civet cats, and vultures . . ." Botting, *Island of the Dragon's Blood,* p. 182.

16. Al-Masudi is quoted in A. Ubaydli, "The Population of Suqutra in the Early Arabic Sources," *Seminar for Arabian Studies 19* (1989): 150.

17. See www.uni-rostock.de/fakult/manafak/biologie/wranik/socotra.

18. Mackintosh-Smith, *Yemen,* p. 223.

19. www.bellona.no/0/08/85/2.html.

20. See http://archive.abcnews.go.com/sections/world/Russia930/index.html. A technical description of a suitcase nuclear weapon can be found at www.nuclearweapon.org/news/dosuitcasenukesexist.html.

21. Victor Hugo, *The Hunchback of Notre Dame* (New York: Tor Classics, 1996), p. 57.

22. Vitaly Naumkin, *Island of the Phoenix: An Ethnographic Study of the People of the Socotra* (Reading, Penn.: Ithaca Press, 1993), p. 205.

23. Botting, *Island of the Dragon's Blood,* p. 163.

24. Naumkin, *Island of the Phoenix,* p. 318.

25. Quoted in Mackintosh-Smith, *Yemen,* p. 207.

26. Naumkin, *Island of the Phoenix,* p. 405.

Dracaena cinnabari

MIKE DAVIS is the father of Roisin, Jack, James, and Cassandra. A MacArthur Fellow, he is the author of *City of Quartz, Ecology of Fear, Magical Urbanism, Dead Cities, Land of the Lost Mammoths*, and other books. He lives in San Diego.

ЖЖ

WILLIAM SIMPSON belongs to Christopher, Conor, Wendy, three dogs, a cat, and a mouse! He has idled away his past seventeen years in Northern Ireland, producing artwork for diverse comic strips, books, and feature films ... with the occasional exhibition thrown in for good measure.